CREW LOVE

THE BLACK MOB

ANTWAN FLOYD SR.

CRIME FICTION MEDIA

A CRIME FICTION MEDIA RELEASE

Crew Love The Black Mob

Copyright © 2011 by Antwan Floyd Sr

Dedicated 2 my sister Est'sherri.

My nieces Classie and Jamise.

My nephews Lil Eddie, Daeron, and David

CONTENTS

HIT OR MISS

The hot, steamy water rained on his flesh from the shower's head. It almost felt like a massage. He relaxed as he closed his eyes and lathered his face with soap. He began to hum Bessie Smith's "Back Water Blues" as he enjoyed the privilege of taking a shower alone. That wasn't a luxury he was normally allotted as a Terre Haute's Federal Prison resident. As he attempted to hit the high note, his singing was cut short as he felt the chicken wire tighten around his neck. His eyes bulged as he dropped the soap, desperately grabbing at his neck trying to get free as he felt his breath getting shorter. He was lifted off his feet as blood ran down his chest.

Struggling and naked, he tried to yell as the soapy water slithered into the corners of his eyes, burning. The assailant grunted aloud and gave one final and ferocious yank; his victim's neck-snapping echoed in his ear. He opened his hands, releasing the chicken wire. The lifeless man's frame hit the cement shower floor with a deadly thud, leaving only the sound of the murderer's heavy breathing and water raining down on his dead frame.

***

The year was 1929. Phil-Good had four years and some odd months in the penitentiary from his five-year bid. His time was getting short, although it had gone by quicker than he thought it would it wasn't going quickly enough. He sat in his room tucked back in the rear of the prison, almost hidden behind the laundry room. It used to be a storage room for the prison's dried foods, but with money and connections, it was now Phil-Good's prison-made apartment. It wasn't home, but it wasn't like a prison either. The meagre space he occupied was more reminiscent of a small living room than that of a state penitentiary. He had a bed on one side of the room, a stove, a personal icebox, a small dinner table, and a leather chair that sat in front of an expensive phonograph player. A guard entered and set a bag of groceries on the table. The scent of garlic, cloves, and sweet sausages filled the room from a pot of spaghetti sauce Phil-Good had simmering on the stove.

"Here are this month's groceries," the portly-sized white guard said dragging his feet as he entered the room.

"Thanks a lot, Sam. There's something for you on the table," Phil-Good said, motioning towards the small stack of money on the table.

"Thank you, Mr. Trenton," Sam said. He picked up the money from the table, stuffed it into his pocket, and exited the cell.

***

Blue Ball and Short Stack both stood outside the Mayflower Baptist Church on 49th and South Parkway as Pastor Barry approached. The flashily dressed two-hundred seventy-five-pound man stood six-feet-seven, looking more like a street pimp than a Pastor of a church. He was light-skinned with deep brown eyes that looked almost black and wore his long-processed hair pulled back in a ponytail.

He wore expensive suits, gold rings on every finger, and on any day, you'd catch him wearing three gold chains at a time. Born and raised in the backwoods of Georgia most of his life, he spoke with a heavy southern drawl. Upon reaching Blue Ball and Short Stack, Pastor Barry shook both men's hands.

He said, "I thank you for all that you have done. Lawd knows the money and clothes you donated will feed and clothe hundreds of needing families."

Blue Ball replied, "It was my pleasure, Pastor. I mean, if we don't help us, who will?"

Blue Ball stood five-feet-eight inches and weighed three-hundred-fifty pounds. Still smooth in his mid-forties, sporting a tailor-made aqua-colored silk suit imported from Italy with matching alligator shoes. Blue Ball was on top of his game when it came to clothes.

"Speaking of us helping us, I still haven't seen the two of you in service yet."

"Don't get me wrong, Pastor, I'm all for helping the kids and prayer and such, but the lord and I got our own arrangement."

Pastor Barry turned up his lip.

"Umm, hmm . . ."

"Didn't I see your picture in the paper the other day, Pastor Barry?" Short Stack asked, changing the subject.

Short Stack, the opposite of his older brother Blue Ball stood five-feet-five inches tall and weighed one-hundred-eighty pounds, all muscle with smooth dark skin. He wasn't hard on the eyes at all."

"Mmm hmm, now I don't pretend to act like I condone Policy or any form of gambling, but we can't trade one evil for another. The police cracking down on all the colored policy banks but aren't touching them mob run banks."

"Like you got to tell us!" Short Stack said with anger in his voice, slamming his fists down on the hood of his car.

"I know every man has a right to earn a living, but if they are going to shut down gambling, shut down everyone operating. They should also furnish these people who will become unemployed with a means of employment." Pastor Barry continued playfully smacking Short Stack on his back to calm him down.

Blue Ball shook his head in disgust.

"It's all politics, Pastor."

"Don't I know it? Politics, corruption, and money. Money from the pockets of poor-colored folks. Don't even get me going!"

"Well, I got a lunch date I need to get to. See you later, Pastor Barry. Blue Ball, I'll catch you later tonight," Short Stack said as he jumped into his Royal Blue 1929 Cadillac. It was fresh off the lot; he only drove the latest models. He had given his 1928 version to a poor family from his old neighbourhood. Short Stack hit the horn twice and zoomed away from the curb.

"I need to get going, too," Blue Ball said, getting into a car that looked like Short Stack's. Starting the engine, he leaned his head out the window.

"Don't forget to call if you need anything and to stop by the department store and take all the supplies you need." He burned rubber, peeling away from the curb and leaving a gust of smoke.

* * *

Phil-Good was a workaholic at heart; he couldn't help himself. He didn't have complete control of the prison's illegal activities the prison, but he had his share. Money and a reputation for shrewdness allotted him the gambling in the prison. Numbers, card games, dice games. Whatever could be betted on, he bet it. Sporting events— it didn't matter to him. He even covered the guard's bets. Phil-Good didn't do it for the money, because shit, he didn't need money. It was all he knew—was good at it, and there ain't nothing else to do.

Same rules, a different environment. Phil-Good still ran all the action. He had a right-hand man who did all his collecting, pay outs, and pulling of the numbers. Peanut McClain, in prison on a robbery bit was a fair man. He and Phil-Good walked down the tier talking as Hollywood approached. Hollywood was what the straight men called a punk. He switched his thin frame around the prison and spoke in a feminine tone. He stopped in front of Peanut McClain, blocking his way. Rocking back and forwards from his heels to his toes, and bouncing in place in a boxer's stance Hollywood said,

"Look, old man, you slept on my number and if you don't want me to scratch your eyes out get me my money, nigga!"

"Look, you he-bitch. If you don't get out my face calling me a cheater and threatening me, I'm going ..." Before Peanut finished his sentence, he caught Hollywood off guard, karate chopping him in the throat. As he gasped for breath, Peanut punched him in the stomach he crumpled to the floor Phil-Good laughed as they both stepped over Hollywood. Now outside on the prison yard, he and Peanut parted ways. Phil-Good looked across the yard and saw Bird and Needles standing with their backs against the wall watching him maneuver his way through the sea of prison inmates. The middle-aged Phil-Good still looked good, easily passing for twenty-nine. Standing at five-feet-ten inches and weighing almost two-hundred pounds, with skin the color of bronze reached the two men and spoke to no one in particular.

"What you got?"

Sporting a scraggly-looking beard, Bird was short, thin, and wore his hair French braided. He had a wide smile with piranha teeth that gouged out of his mouth. Bird was the most dangerous man in the penitentiary. He had been in out-of-state and federal facilities since his teenage years. He was the leader of the biggest black gang in the prison, *The Bloody Feathers!*

"You know that hit in the shower this morning was meant for you, don't you?" Bird uttered the words in a hushed tone.

"Damn, it's fucked up how they left Roderick ... If I wouldn't have let that brother get my private shower time that would have been me laid out. What you got?" Phil-Good says as he placed a cigarette between his lips.

"Not sure, but I'm gonna find out. The word so far is that it might be Der Orden."

"You know why these red-neck fucks pulling this shit?"

"I ain't sure if it's them or not, just take it easy, brother."

"Piranha gonna watch your back 'til this thing blows over," Needles said, sounding more like an order than a request.

He had a habit of giving orders; he couldn't help it. Being a leader came naturally. Needles was second in command of The Bloody Feathers. This was a huge accomplishment for him, being only sixteen years old. He stood five-feet-eight inches and was of average size.

He wasn't a bodybuilder, but he had a toned muscular frame, dark-skinned with a Mustache and goatee. Needles was short-tempered and was known throughout the prison as someone you did not fuck with! Even the guards bestowed him as much respect as they did the warden, if not more.

Phil-Good looked over Needles' crudeness.

Phil-Good said, "Look Bird, I appreciate you trying to look out for me and everything, but I don't need Piranha or nobody else babysitting me."

Bird pounded his fists in his palm with aggression and annoyance. "Phil, ain't no time for that macho bullshit. We all know you a tough ass nigga! But you can't walk this yard by yourself with these Der Orden muthafuckas trying to stick a shank in you!"

Phil-Good bit into his bottom lip, his muscles tightened as he clenched both fists. "You ain't gonna let up on this shit, are you?"

Stone-faced, Bird replied, "It's either you let Piranha watch your back or I do the job for Der Orden!"

Phil-Good motioned Piranha, who had now joined the men against the wall, to follow him. Piranha was one of the oldest members of The Bloody Feathers He had fists like bricks and had once broken a man's neck from the impact of punching him in the face. He got the name Piranha (a joke in itself) because his entire top row of teeth was missing.

Phil-Good said, "Let's go, man."

They walked through the crowd of men who parted like the Red Sea, making room for Phil- Good and his obvious bodyguard to pass through.

***

Blue Ball pulled the shiny new car up to the curb in front of a number's bank he managed on 60th and South Parkway. He parked and walked into the apartment building. Empty candy wrappers and soda bottles littered the filthy blood-stained floors. Walking up the stairs he grabbed a hold of the old wooden stair banister it was so brittle it felt as though it would crush underneath his touch. Walking down the hall he could hear conversations from the residents in the different apartments the walls were so thin. In apartment 4B a mother fusses at her child to hurry and get dressed for his doctor's appointment, in apartment 5B he could hear loud screams of what he only imagined was a lustful passionate couple having sex, upon reaching the apartment 6B the screams he heard coming from this apartment were anything but passionate. The yells were ear-shattering and dug into your skin it was so wretched the hairs on the back of his hand stood up. Unlocking the door, he stepped in and closed the door. He scanned the room Boy-Boy and Little Larry had Uncle Everett sitting in a chair with his face bashed in and bleeding all over himself. Uncle Everett was not Blue Ball's uncle; it was a nickname that everyone called him. He was a mess. His left eye was barely holding on to its socket, looking like a piece of over-tenderized meat! No one spoke Blue Ball nodded at Boy-Boy and Lil Larry acknowledging the two men.

Uncle Everett let out a low hacking sound as he struggled to breathe because it was difficult to do so with broken ribs. Blue Ball hated this part of the game. He always did. You could not tell that by looking at him; he never let any emotions show. Since he was getting older in age, he felt he had to be even more cruel than necessary—to keep 'wanna-be-bad' guys from even thinking about pulling it with him. Uncle Everett had been working at this bank for over five years. Blue Ball liked the old guy. He had always looked at the man as a surrogate father.

Nevertheless, Blue Ball could not let this slide. Uncle Everett had been stealing money for over three months that Blue Ball knew of three thousand dollars a night. That was what Blue Ball had stumbled onto. No telling how much he had stolen over the past five years. Blue Ball felt he had to pass judgment quickly and fiercely. Boy-Boy and Little Larry were two of his all-purpose guys, he could've easily let them handle this for him. Blue Ball not only wanted to get the word out to other people not to fuck with his money or they would be dealt with, but he also wanted to let his young cronies know what they had coming if they decided to dip into his pockets. He looked Uncle Everett in the eyes, yanking his head back. "Please Blue... whatever it is you think I did man I ain't do let's talk this out." Uncle Everett begged in a muffled tone as he gurgled on his own blood. He spat up his blood as he hacked and coughed blood ran down his chin. Blue Ball's eyes flashed a sign of empathy it was too late now, no turning back besides what would his soldiers think? He yanked Uncle Everett's head back neither of the men had seen Blue Ball pull the razor they just saw Uncle Everett's legs jerk and twitch as Blue Ball cut his throat from ear to ear.

* * *

It had been almost twenty years since Pastor Barry had moved to Chicago. He had no relatives here and no friends. Until he became a member of the church and later became the Pastor, no one knew who Pastor Barry was or where he came from. Night services had wrapped for the night. Pastor Barry was taking notes from a scripture in the Bible preparing for tomorrow night's service when he heard a noise outside his office.

Pastor Barry, far from being a cowardly man had no true reason to believe he was in any real danger. He closed his Bible and walked out to where he held the congregation. When he turned the corner to enter the sanctuary, he was surprised to see a single man sitting in the front row smoking a cigar.

Pastor Barry froze in his tracks as if he had looked eyes to eyes with Lucifer himself! A whirl of smoke slowly ascended to the ceiling of the church. The small man sitting in the front row with his feet propped up was a man that Pastor Barry had not seen in almost twenty years.

Paul Anthony came from the same small town in Georgia that Pastor Barry came from. Only back then he did not go by Pastor Stanley Barry. He was known as Stanley Trudeau, a half-breed mulatto boy half-Colored half-French. His mother was poor white trash who lived with the Colored folks on their side of town. His father, whom he never knew anyway, had long gone before he was even walking. By the time Stanley had reached his late teens, he had been in more street fights than he remembered.

People were constantly talking down about his mother. One day, when Stanley came home early from school, is having been kicked-out again for fighting, he walked in on a man raping his mother. As he heard the wretched screams of pain and humiliation escape his mother's mouth, a lump formed in his throat and tears welled in his eyes. Stanley snatched the man by his neck lifting him from his feet he slammed the man against the wall. He squirmed and struggled to get free clawing at Stanley his eyes bulging from his face. Stanley's mother screamed for him to stop. "You're going to kill him!" She screamed as she covered herself with a sheet. Stanley ignored his mother as he continued squeezing, the man's legs kicked uncontrollably as life escaped from his body. Stanley squeezed until no more life was left in his mother's attacker's body. Stanley felt the last breath of air escape from the man's frame. Stanley threw the man against the wall like a ragdoll his head hit the old wood floor Stanley watched as the blood oozed from his head. Stanley left that night in fear for his life. The man he had killed was nobody important, but the men who would avenge his death were anything but nobodies!

The Anthony family was a family of one girl and eight boys, ranging in age from twelve years old up to thirty years old. At least half had spent some time or another on a prison chain gang. Some for murder, but mostly for assault. The man Stanley had killed was their only sister's husband.

Stanley begged his mother to go with him, but she refused, and he said he would not leave if she would not go with him. She told him he was no longer welcomed in her home and if the Anthony boys were going to kill him, it would not be in her home in front of her eyes! He hopped a train heading North and ended up in Kansas City, Missouri, never to return. Two years later, a mysterious string of murders began occurring one by one. The Anthony boys began to have weird accidents resulting in their deaths!

Starting with the youngest, Troy was fourteen, and one day while out in the fields Troy had been found dead. He had been trampled to death, at least that's what everyone had assumed since he had mule tracks all over his overalls. Two weeks later, two more brothers died. Their pickup truck had stalled on the railroad tracks and neither got out in time before the train tore the truck to shreds. Over the next six months, more strange incidents occurred, knocking the Anthony boys off one by one. All except one.

What no one knew is that those incidents were far from being accidents. Stanley, without anyone knowing had been sneaking in and out of town killing the Anthony boys, and on his last trip, he saw Paul Anthony, he was being hauled off to prison for the long haul for killing a white man. He never thought he would get out. In the back of the wagon, they made eye contact and Paul Anthony smiled a deadly smile as the cart pulled away. Pastor Barry shook off the trip down memory lane, "Can I help you, sir?" He asked looking at Paul Anthony out the corner of his eye as he busied himself picking up loose Bibles.

"Yes, you can. I'm looking for *Stan-lay True-dough*," Paul Anthony said in a strong country accent.

"Don't know a Trudeau." Pastor Barry says as he continued picking up the loose Bibles, trying his best to avoid direct eye contact.

"I was told I could find him here in this church."

"I'm the Pastor of this church and I know most of the congregation and I can't say that I don't know a Trudeau. Maybe your source was mistaken."

"Maybe, sorry for taking up your time, Pastor. What did you say your name was?"

"Barry. Pastor Barry. Sorry, I couldn't have been more help to you."

"It's alright, Pastor. You've helped me more than you know."

Paul Anthony, although older in age had the same features he had, had over twenty years ago. Before exiting the church, he smiled at Pastor Barry with the same grimacing smile as he had done in the back of the prison wagon. It sent a chill up the Pastor's spine. Pastor Barry watched the man leave and became frightened, not that he feared for his own life, but he feared for his soul. He had made a promise to God to never kill again. He wondered if it came down to it would he be able to keep his word to God!"

* * *

Short Stack and Monique sat at a table in Sylvia's Soul Food Emporium on 29th and South LaSalle drinking iced tea and making small talk. Short Stack reached out and took Monique's hand.

"What are you going to get, baby?" He asked as he placed her hand on his lips and kissed it.

Monique was still looking at the menu. "I don't know. I don't have a taste for this."

"What do you have a taste for?"

"I don't know. You are the one who wanted to come here. what do you want to talk to me about?" She asked staring into Short Stack's eyes with a pure look of innocence that often made Short Stack's heart melt.

"I got a surprise for you!" Short Stack said with a nervous smile on his face.

Monique beamed her hazel eyes lit up with anticipation. She was not the young woman she once was. But being in her early forties, she was still better looking than women half her age. Monique was an attractive light-skinned woman of average height with beautiful sandy brown colored hair down her back. Her youthful face and curvy shape left men commenting that she was still fine.

"A surprise for me?" she asked, filled with perkiness in her voice.

"You know how I feel about you, right?" he asked, not revealing any form of emotion.

Monique hated when he did this. She had no problem reading men, but Short Stack was a feather of another color.

"Baby, yeah I feel the same way about ..."

Short Stack held up his hand, cutting her off mid-sentence. "That's why as a token of my love for you, would you ..."

"Baby, yes! Yes, of course, I will!" Monique blurted out, cutting Short Stack off mid-sentence.

Short Stack stared back at her confused and reached into his breast pocket and pulled out an envelope. "I thought you might be happy, but I never expected this," Short Stack said.

Monique spoke in a disappointing tone. "*What's that?*"

"That's my surprise. It's the deed to this place."

"Awww." Monique was now filled with disappointment.

Short Stack not missing the upset look that covered her face asked, "What? It's yours. You going to own your own diner!"

"Hmph!" Monique could not help but show her disapproval. They had been together for over twenty years, and she had given up hope of ever marrying him. Just as it seemed he was about to put her waiting to an end, he snatched it all away from her again.

Short Stack didn't understand the reason for the animosity. Impatiently tapping his nails on the diner table his forehead wrinkled, "What? You don't want it?"

"No, it's not that, but when you said surprise, I thought you were going to ..."

"I was going to what?" He blurted out cutting her off.

Monique's feelings were hurt. She folded her arms and sighed. "Nothing, let's order."

Short Stack pounded his hands on the table knocking over a glass of water. "Fuck that. What's the problem? You want the diner or what?" He couldn't understand how she could be so unappreciative. She had worked there damn near her whole life, even when he told her she could quit, and he would care for both. She could have something that was hers, but that was a woman, never satisfied.

Monique sucked her teeth raising an eyebrow talked to Short Stack through clenched teeth. "Don't be fucking cussing at me, Negro. Look, it was a nice thought, but I can't accept the diner!"

"Why the fuck not?"

"It's too much. I can't, okay? Drop it. Thank you, but no thank you."

Leaning his seat back on two legs and picking the dirt from underneath his nails with a steak knife he snarled at Monique. "Woman, you crazy as hell!"

"If I'm so crazy, why the fuck are you still with my crazy ass?"

"I don't know maybe I'm crazier than you is!" Monique scoots herself from the table and forcefully snatches her handbag from the table knocking over a chair as she heads towards the door. Never turning to look back at Short Stack she says.

"Look, I ain't hungry no more. Take me home, okay!" She snatches the door open and turns towards Short Stack glaring through him with eyes of fire.

Short Stack shook his head in disbelief. "Here go the bullshit!"

"I ain't trying to get into all that. Take me home. Can you do that for me, Obadiah?"

Short Stack stood and headed for the door. "Let's go, man!"

* * *

Jermaine Lloyd and his wife, Tania both sat talking in his office he had built in the back of the Palm Inn when the telephone rang.

Jermaine picked up the receiver. "Hello."

The voice on the other end of the telephone is Royal Talker, an old friend, who was once a heavy figure in the black underworld. Now he's a former gangster turned politician.

Jermaine continues. "Yeah, how's it going, Royal?"

"Good, good, listen ..." Royal said frantically.

Tania blurted out, "Tell Royal I said hi."

"Tania says hi."

"Tell her hi, but listen, I called to tell you I got word that the sheriff is on his way down to serve you a summons!" Royal said, trying to get it all out as quickly as possible.

"A summons for what?" Jermaine yelled.

"To appear in court for tax evasion. Thought I would give you a heads up."

"Thanks a lot, Royal, I'll be in touch," Jermaine said, slamming down the telephone. He rushed over to the painting of himself and his wife on their wedding day and removed it from the wall to reveal a safe.

"What happened, baby?" Tania asked, looking confused.

"We got to go!" He shouted as he spun the dial to the combination, then yanked the door open.

"Go? Go where?" She asked with a slight look of fear across her face.

Jermaine began throwing bundles of money on the desk and slammed the door of the safe closed.

"Anywhere out of Chicago. Come on, put that shit in a bag. Let's go!"

Tania jumped up frantically and picked up the trashcan next to the desk.

"What happened, baby?" She asked as she began throwing the bundles of cash into the trashcan.

"I got a summons to go to court. They're trying to charge me with tax evasion. It's going to be that whole Phil-Good situation all over again."

"You sure? It might not turn out like that. Do you think running is the right idea? "She managed to get out as she pulled the trash liner filled with money from the can. Jermaine grabbed her by the wrist and pulled her towards the door.

"It might not be the right idea, but it's the best I got right now. I'll sort my legal situation out with Carlin over the phone!" Carlin was an old friend and the best criminal defense attorney in the state.

* * *

After dropping Monique at home, Short Stack thought he would check in with the boys and see what everyone was up to. As he pulled up to the Palm Inn and parked behind Blue Ball's car, he got out and climbed into the backseat of his brother's car, and slammed the door closed. Blue Ball sipped on a bottle of whiskey, and he passed the bottle back to Short Stack. "What's up man?" Short Stack asked as he placed the bottle to his lips and guzzled the liquor.

"Shit." Blue Ball said nonchalantly.

"Umm ...Who up in there?"

"Shit, I don't know. I just pulled up, too. Look man, I'm tired."

"Long day?"

"No, I mean of *the life,* the rackets, everything." Blue Ball banged his fists on the steering wheel.

"Tired my ass! Are you burned out? Go down to the islands for a few weeks and you'll be good when you get back."

"Naw, it's more than that, little brother. I mean I'm tired. Shit, not just my body and mind. I mean my soul is literally tired." He exclaimed grabbing at his chest.

"What then?"

Blue Ball wiped imaginary dust from his hands. "Wiping my hands clean."

"And do what?"

"Religion."

Short Stack began laughing.

"Get the fuck out of here. Religion. What, like preaching?"

"Yeah, that's exactly what I mean."

"What's your angle? I know it's a scam behind this somewhere. Those churches are tax-free dollars, right? Now you are going ..."

"Naw, naw, naw, little brother. This is all on the up and up. No scams. God told me it was time."

"*God* told you?" Short Stack asked, not believing the words that were coming from his brother's mouth.

"Yeah, God told me."

"Look Blue, you my big brother. I love you and support you in everything you do, but I hope God ain't told you it was time for me."

"It's not my place to tell you. When it's time, you'll know. I thought you should hear it from me first."

"I appreciate that, but what about your cut of the businesses?"

"Donate my portion of the profit to Pastor Barry."

"Whatever you say, man."

* * *

Short Stack needed to relax. He went over to his friend's house to get away and get Monique and Blue Ball off his mind. She stayed in a modest looking two flat at 6157 Ebrhart. He parked and walked into the unit, which he unlocked with the spare key she had given him for emergencies. Her name was Samantha Harris, the complete physical opposite of Monique.

She was darker in complexion, had short curly hair, was tall, and weighed a hundred pounds even. She was pretty and had a sexy figure to have such a thin frame. Although he kept their relationship a secret from Monique, nothing sexual between the two of them ever happened.

That had nothing to do with Samantha; she had liked Short Stack from the start. But Short Stack had an undying loyalty towards Monique and Samantha respected that. Samantha had a six-year-old son that Short Stack was fond of. He often took the boy to the horse tracks with him and on his pick-ups throughout the city. He and Samantha had a special friendship that he and Monique would never have. He sat on the beige-colored couch, removed his gun from the front of his pants, and laid it on the coffee table. Pink and yellow paint covered the walls, wall-to-wall hardwood floors that shone to perfection. Samantha always kept a spotless home. He walked across the room and turned on the record player. Returning to his seat on the couch he heard Samantha moving about in the kitchen. The rest of the house was particularly quiet her little boy must be over to her mothers he thought as he inhaled the sweet scent of whatever it was Samantha had on the stove in the kitchen his stomach growled. Samantha entered and handed Short Stack a plate of smoked ribs and greens. He took the plate as she sat down next to him and laid her head on his shoulder. Her hair smelled good, she laid her head back and looked up into his eyes lovingly.

"Everything all right?" she asked, sensing he had something on his mind.

"Everything cool, "He said, stuffing the hot food into his mouth.

She thought to herself, *I would ask one more time. If he says nothing is wrong, I will leave it alone.* Although their relationship was platonic, she still could not stomach discussing Monique and the problems they went through. She asked in the most genuine tone she could muster.

"You sure?"

"Monique is ungrateful as hell sometimes!" he managed to get out between bites of food.

"What do you mean?"

"I bought her a gift today and she got an attitude."

Samantha held her breath, she caught a hot flash she hated feeling jealous, but she did. *Monique doesn't know a thing about taking care of a man as good as Short Stack*, she thought as she held her composure." Are you sure that's all to it?" She asked. Being a woman herself, she knew there had to be more to it. Women don't get angry over getting gifts. That's asshole backward.

"Look, can I stay the night?"

"You know it's not a problem, you're always welcome here. Will you sleep in the room this time?"

"Naw, the couch is cool," he said as he finished his ribs and greens. She lifts her head from his shoulder and got up from the couch going into her room and slamming the door closed.

* * *

Phil-Good and Piranha walked the prison yard en route to meet with Peanut to discuss more mistakes he's been making with the bets he's been collecting. Piranha attempted to walk around the court of a basketball game that was being played. Phil-Good didn't break stride, he marched right through the court full of men disregarding their game. Piranha knew it was uncalled-for trouble, but it was his job to protect Phil-Good, and if Phil-Good was in the wrong or not that's what he would do. The men stopped and stared as they all scowled at the two passing by. A few of the angry men shouted and cursed, but none would pursue the issue any further. None of the men wanted problems with Piranha, let alone The Bloody Feathers. Phil-Good knew it was wrong too, but this place was getting to him. The death threats, Piranha following him all the time, and the twenty-four-seven, three-sixty-five days of nothing but men. Plus, fuck em all is what he thought. Any one of these whining bitches could've been the one who put Roderick to sleep in that shower. Before they were completely off the court, Phil-Good's head jerked from the impact of being smacked in the face with a basketball. Dazed but not out, Phil-Good struck out toward the man nearest to him. He obviously didn't throw the ball, but someone had to pay. Phil-Good punched the man in the face, making his nose bleed. The man stepped back, gripping his bloody face. Piranha immediately joined in the brawl, fighting three men at a time, and was getting the better of the three men. Some of the men who were playing the game scattered and others who were watching the game rushed over and formed a circle to watch the brawl. More members of The Bloody Feathers joined in the fight, which now had more than thirty men fighting. The loud prison siren rang out. Guards from overhead appeared, surrounding the men below and aiming rifles into the crowd. The men hit the ground, covering their heads as prison guards rushed the yard attempting to gain control over the situation. Phil-Good lies face down covering his head bleeding from the mouth staring at a dead man two feet away with a prison-made knife sticking out the side of his rib cage.

* * *

Twenty-one-year-old Lil Larry had been working for Blue Ball for almost a year now and it paid well. He had forced himself into this work. He could put someone on ice and do it in a cold way, but he knew deep down inside it wasn't who he was. He never had any ill will nor second thoughts about what he did to people, but he was starting to have nightmares. He would be working with Short Stack now and he knew working for him with his short temper he would be a busy man. He knew he would have to quit this shit soon or find a way to shake that shit off.

He walked into the Soul Food restaurant at 29th South LaSalle and had a seat. Leaning back in his seat, he closed his eyes. He hadn't had any real sleep in almost three days. As he was dozing off, he was tapped on the shoulder. Out of pure reflex, he reached for the gun in his belt.

Monique, not missing the gesture, but not afraid either, told him, "Calm down Mister, I'm just bringing you a menu."

Lil Larry let go of his weapon. Feeling embarrassed he took the menu. "Thank you."

Now Lil Larry wasn't a ladies' man, but he was never at a loss for words either, but Monique had taken his breath away. It wasn't like it was their first time seeing one another, but she was the boss's girl so their conversation was limited to hello, goodbye and can I get that for you? Although she had about twenty-plus years on him, he had made up his mind that one day she would be his. If she knew it or not, they would be together.

* * *

Danny sat at his desk with his feet propped up leaning back in his chair with eyes closed. He daydreamed about where he would take his new empire. He had just gotten off the phone with his girlfriend, Apricot and everything was in place to advance to the next stage of his plan. Everything wasn't as smooth as he would've liked, but it was moving. He would prove to his father in prison that he was man enough to carry the responsibility of the business on his shoulders. It would be harder now with Uncle Jermaine on the lam, and Uncle Blue Ball retiring, but he still had his uncles, Short Stack and Rodney Pipe, plus his right-hand man Randy, so shit should flow smoothly. The telephone rang. He opened his eyes and answered on the first ring. He didn't recognize the voice on the other end of the phone that had identified himself as Charlie. Charlie had told him that he would pay—he and his family would all pay. Danny disregarded the threat and hung up. He had to pick up Apricot from the airport in a few hours. He leaned back in his seat once again and closed his eyes. He would get a quick nap in before her plane arrived.

* * *

Randy drove along 42nd and Wabash until he came across the address he was looking for. He parked his car and walked into his mother's home. She always kept the door unlocked. Everyone in the neighborhood knew the Anderson's and all loved Ms. Anderson. The local boys on the block always mowed her grass in the summer and shoveled her walkway in the winter. All out of respect. Not only for Ms. Anderson but also to stay in Randy's good graces.

"Hey Mama!" he yelled out as he always did when he came into the house.

"You ain't got to do all that hollering, boy, I ain't going deaf."

Randy walked into the kitchen where his mother was sitting at the table splitting fresh peas from her garden. She still got along well for her age. She still drove herself to the market, although Randy did not approve of it. She cooked all her own meals and cleaned around the house.

Randy hired a cleaning woman to come in twice a week to keep his mother from working so hard. She still did what she wanted to do anyway. Randy kissed his mother on the cheek and looked into the refrigerator, pulling out a jug of milk. Removing the cap, he was about to put the bottle to his lips. He looked over at his mother with her eyes trained on him.

"I ain't gonna do it, Mama!" he said, getting a glass from the cabinet.

She snapped. "I know damn well you ain't. Nigga, you know better than that. I hope you don't do that fool shit when you go over to women's homes! Got them girls thinking I ain't teach you shit!"

"Look Mama, I got a glass, okay?" he said, filling the glass up and placing the jug back into the refrigerator.

"You heard what I said, boy?"

"Yes ma'am, but I don't deal with women that's too particular about that type of stuff."

"Well, you need to be more *particular* about the women you deal with."

"Yes ma'am."

"You stopping by for dinner, baby?"

"I doubt it, Mama. You sure you don't want to go to the wedding?"

"Thank you, baby, but a couple of the girls are stopping by to play bridge tonight, but I'll put a plate up for you. You stop by and get it tomorrow."

Randy snatched a piece of cake off the plate on the table, downed his milk, and kissed his mother on the cheek then darted out of the kitchen yelling, "See you tomorrow, Ma!"

"You be careful out there, boy!"

He yelled back, "Yes ma'am."

* * *

THE RECONSTRUCTION PERIOD

T he banquet hall of the Reason's Golf Course was packed full of people white and colored. The crew was all there Danny, Randy, Jermaine, Rodney Pipe, and the rest. Phil-Fine stood holding his glass as he tapped it with a fork to get the attention of the people talking amongst themselves. The soft conversation became silent.

Phil-Fine had grown into an impeccable young man. At six feet even, two hundred pounds, (give or take a few pounds) wavy hair, and a goatee he kept groomed, he would be the ideal lady's man if he chose to be.

Phil-Fine said, "Attention, attention everyone. Let's get this thing started."

Setting his glass of wine and fork back on the table he cleared his throat and continued. "First of all, let me take this opportunity to say thank you to Reasons Golf Course for the use of their beautiful golf course and the city of Gary for accepting us with a warm welcome. Mayor Barney Payton, City Councilman Bob Andes, and the most important man here, Policy King Lil Walter Ready. Uh, uh, with no disrespect to the city officials, Mr. Mayor!" The room burst into laughter.

"None taken," Mayor Payton said, laughing himself.

Picking up where he left off Phil-Fine continued, "We got Kings from right here in Indiana, Chicago, Cleveland, Detroit, Peoria, St. Louis, St. Paul, and Harlem!"

Rodney Pipe yelled out. "Yeah, everybody up in here!"

"Are you gonna get on with it or what?"Jermaine asked, joking with Phil-Fine.

"I just wanted to say thank you to everyone for coming out and celebrating this wonderful day with us, me and my new wife sharing our vows, Everybody eat good, drink good, and party hard!"

With that cue, the band started playing as couples began rushing to the dance floor. Phil-Fine took his new wife's hand into his and pulled her close, planting a long passionate kiss across her full heart-shaped lips. The room erupted into applause and cheers.

Danny leaned over in his seat and whispered in Randy's ear, "Meet you over at the spot." He still needed to pick Apricot up from the airport.

* * *

Apricot stepped off the plane at the Decatur Airport in Decatur, Ill. A sexy, dark skin complexioned Jamaican woman in her early twenties. At five feet nine inches tall, weighing one hundred forty pounds, with medium-sized breasts, and an ass you could see from the front, she walked over to the baggage claim and picked up a suitcase. Two airport baggage handlers escorted her to the arrival area, pushing carts with three duffel bags a piece on them.

She led them outside where Danny was waiting. He kissed Apricot and then opened the passenger door. Once she sat safely inside, he closed the door and placed the luggage and the duffel bags in the trunk. Tipping the two men, he then returned to his seat and pulled off.

Danny looked down admiring Apricot's thick legs. He looks into her eyes that were trained on him.

"You have a nice flight?"

She answered back in a Jamaican accent, "It did alright a likkle' bumpy still."

"Listen doll, I don't want you making no more runs."

"Ah nuh nutin'still...comin' in like takin' candy from one likkle pickney." she replied as she ran her smooth dark hands down the side of his face. Danny smiled.

"I'm not folding on this shit. It's too dangerous. Besides, the next shit I got coming through gonna be too big. Your brother got a man with his own plane flying it in."

"So wha di' big man, 'affe sey bout' dat?"

Danny instantly became upset, accelerating the gas his nose flared up. He didn't like to appear as if he weren't in charge. As if he had to get the okay to make shit happen, although he knew he did need the okay, he still felt in his heart he should be running things. It only angered him more when others didn't look at him in the same way as he saw himself.

"Don't you worry your pretty little head 'bout Uncle Jermaine, I got this in the bag," he replied brushing her off. They both rode in silence for the remainder of the ride, twenty minutes later he was back in Chicago pulling into the junkyard he owned. A car pulled in behind them. Danny got out of the car and opened the trunk. He removed one of the duffel bags and walked to the car parked behind him. The car behind his is Randy's. He handed him the duffel bag.

"Fresh from Jamaica. Randy held the bag as Danny unzipped it and placed his nose near the lime green of Jamica's finest marijuana sniffing the potent hemp, the scent filled his nostrils. A sinister smile crept across Randy's face. This a sample." Danny zipped the bag back closed slapped hands with Randy and climbed back into the driver's seat of his car. Leaning his head out the window he says. "Stop by the spot later to get the rest. Be careful and see you back at the wedding reception."

* * *

Bird sat in the visiting area across from his wife. She was gorgeous. A Spoonful stood at four eleven with a brown skin complexion, long curly hair, green eyes, perfect white teeth, and a sexy petite frame. They had been married since he was sixteen and she was twelve. They had a son together, in fact, that was the only reason she was there visiting. She loved Bird to death and although he spent most of their marriage locked up; she never divorced him and had never slept with another man.

She hated coming to the prison and looking into the eyes of the men there. She did not like what she saw. Yeah, some had the look of stone-cold killers, but most looked like sad beaten-down men— even worst, sad beaten-down colored men.

A Spoonful looked across the table at the man she loved whom she still considered the head of her household with a solemn expression. "Lil Percy acting a fool again!"

"What is it now?" Bird sighed and rubbed his temples as he felt a headache coming on.

"They threatening to kick him out of school again."

"Did you tell him what I said?"

"Do you think you *scare* him from inside here?"

"He gonna see!"

"Come on, Percy, be for real. We need to come up with a serious solution before this boy end up dead or up in here where you are."

He took a deep breath. "I'll handle it."

"Handle it how Percy?"

Too much contact between the inmates and the visitors was prohibited but the little contact they did have with one another Bird enjoyed it. He brushed his rough calloused index finger across the top of her smooth silky hand, across her knuckle down her finger stopping at her fingernail. She smiled. "How are you doing?" he said changing the subject.

She hated when he did that, but she did not come down often so she went with the flow not to ruin the visit.

"I'm fine. I started a new job bagging groceries."

"That's good, baby. You have been getting the money I have been sending?"

"Yeah, it's been helping out a lot, but you ain't got to ..."

He interrupted. "I ain't got to what? Support my family the best way I can. I mean shit; y'all still my family, ain't y'all?"

She smiled. "Yeah baby, I love you."

"I love you, too, and don't worry 'bout Lil Percy. Consider it taken care of!"

"I think he gonna be okay for a little while."

"Why did you say that?"

"You know that piece you left with me to take care of myself?"

"Yeah."

"After I got tired of talking and pleading and yelling, I had to do something. And he too big to be whooping with a belt, so I shot at him."

Bird laughed. "You ain't hurt him, did you, baby?"

She laughed. "Naw just scared some sense into him."

* * *

Later that night at the wedding reception, Danny and the rest of the crew drank cognac and joked with Phil Fine.

"What was so important that you needed all of us here instead of getting on that plane and taking that fine-ass wife of yours on that honeymoon?" Danny joked.

Phil-Fine walked around the room looking into the eyes of all the men there whom he respected and admired. "I know it's going to come as a big surprise to everyone, but when it comes time for me to come back from my honeymoon, I'm stepping away from the business."

"The little lady breaking you down, huh?" Short Stack said teasing Phil-Fine.

"Naw, it's not that."

"What is it, little brother? You could've waited to tell us this," Danny said, trying to get to the core of the announcement.

"I'm going on a spiritual pilgrimage."

"A spiritual who?" Danny repeated.

"A spiritual pilgrimage," Phil-Fine repeated.

"Where's all of this coming from?"

"Sandra and I need to find ourselves."

"Find y'all selves. Now don't you sound silly?" Danny said, looking at Phil-Fine with disappointment in his eyes.

Big James was something like an elder statesman when it came to running numbers, should've retired years ago but the game was still in him so he kept hustling. "I think it's cool. How long are you talking about?" He asks looking like a proud father.

"Six months, a year. I don't know how long, but I know we can't come back until we're complete."

"Until you're complete? Complete with what?" Danny asked, becoming agitated.

"Complete mentally and spiritually," Short Stack replied.

"Where is this spiritual voyage taking place?"

"Egypt, then I don't know. Maybe Tibet, wherever the winds carry us!"

"I'm supposed to be taking care of you while Pop's gone," Danny said like the concerned older brother he is.

"I'll be all right."

"What the fuck do you mean 'I'll be all right'. You talking about some bullshit voyage," Danny blurted out, showing his frustration with Phil-Fine.

"Danny, be cool man!" Blue Ball tried to calm down the angry young man.

"Naw! Fuck that, Uncle Blue Ball. Phil man, go on your little trip or whatever and get your head right, but don't be talking that yang-yang when you get back."

Phil-Fine didn't need his brother's approval, but he did want it and it felt good being sent off with his blessings. He hugged his brother. He knew when he returned he would not be getting back into the business. Phil-Fine just wasn't as *street* as Danny was and probably never would be. He didn't want the responsibility of running a multi-million dollar operation.

Phil-Fine smiled like a young schoolboy before saying. "Thanks, man. I love you, but I was going regardless!"

Danny tried to hold back the smile and hold on to his stern facial expression but a wide smile crept across his face. "I know." He says as he grabs his brother and throws him in a bear hug.

The men erupted into laughter.

***

Lil Percy was coming out of the neighborhood pool hall talking and laughing with two of his friends. They had beaten a few suckers out of their rent money in a game of pool. It was about time for him to get home. His mother would be expecting him. He should have been coming in from school at this time. Her shooting at him didn't mean shit. *No time for that school shit, it was money to be made*, Lil Percy thought. *I'm not gonna make that shit sitting in some bullshit class.* He put his share of the money in his pocket. A vagrant leaned against the wall clutching a bottle of liquor with a cigarette butt perched between his lips. The trench coat he wore was tattered and stained. Underneath his left eye, his facial skin held a scar in his skin looking like a permanent black eye. He approached Lil Percy still clutching the bottle, and called out from across the street.

"Ain't you supposed to be in school, boy?"

Lil Percy towered at six feet five and had a natural strength that came with his two-hundred seventy pounds. He ignored the middle-aged stranger approaching him. And so did his friends, who were not tiny either. The three young boys were practically neck and neck in weight and height. The three boys pegged the stranger as an old drunk since the neighborhood was infested with them. Once close enough to stand eyes to eye, the man told Lil Percy, "How you boys do today? Break me off a cut of the day's profit."

The three boys dismissed the question and laughed. The man began laughing with them. Percy looked down at the stranger.

"You better go head-on before we whoop yo' old ass!"

The stranger grinned, then reached up and grabbed Lil Percy by the back of the neck with his left arm. He smashed the boy's face with the elbow of his right arm, crushing his nose.

Blood leaped from his face as the crunching from his nose bones echoed in his ear. The other two boys went into action. The one nearest him punched the stranger on the side of his head. The stranger's frame smacked the cement. The stranger had known from years of street fights and prison brawls that when you're outnumbered do not let 'em get you down and keep your back to the wall.

He hadn't done either, underestimating the young boys and thinking they might get the best of him. They knew the rules, too: When you get a nigga down, don't let him up. As instinctual as breathing, the two boys' pummeled the stranger with kicks to his stomach and back. By this time Lil Percy had regained his composure and was eager to get in on the fight. He ran over to continue fighting, helping his boys get a few more kicks in. The stranger took the blows without balling up. Somehow he made it to his feet and removed a wooden bat hidden in his leather trench coat. This caught the three boys by surprise.

The first swing he got off broke the boy closest to him down as he went to work on his knees. The boy let out a loud ear-shattering yell and crumpled to the ground like a ball of crumpled-up paper. Lil Percy and his other friend both took a step back but didn't run. Not wanting to take their eyes off the lunatic with the bat, they both let their eyes dart around the streets looking for a weapon to defend themselves. *A brick, a stick, a broken bottle, anything shit,* Lil Percy thought to himself. *As dirty as these streets usually be when I need some shit ain't shit around!* Before he finished his thought, the stranger finished his rampage by splitting his other friend's forearm. The bone ripped right through his flesh!

He dropped to his knees gripping his new wound as blood ran through his fingers. The stranger stood clutching the blood-covered bat with a wild look in his eyes, and slob running from the corners of his mouth. He stares into Lil Percy's eyes.

"I like that in y'all. Y'all ain't run like some little bitches. But I still need that paper run that!"

Lil Percy readied himself to fight with the crazy old man with the bat, showing no fear Lil Percy ran up arms swinging yelling.

"Man, fuck you if you gonna rob me um gonna be broke down I ain't just giving you my shit!"

He swung the bat hitting Lil Percy in the stomach he dropped to his knees and vomited. The stranger went through the three boys' pockets and took the money; one of the three also had a gun wedged in the front of his pants, and he took that too.

"I guess y'all lil niggas is honorable; kept it a street fight, but I wouldn't have did no shit like that."

Standing over the three boys clutching the blood-covered bat, he knelt down so that he was at eye level with Lil Percy. He burped, and the foul scent of chitterlings mixed with stale beer flooded Lil Percy's nostrils. He cringed. The stranger said, "Get to know this face, I'm Chuck. Ya Daddy sent me to whoop yo' young ass. That's why you ain't get it the same as yo' little punk-ass friends. But if I catch you up here again or I hear from your daddy you ain't going to school, I'm gone whoop yo punk ass *again!*"

***

It was 5:30 in the morning as Danny came staggering out of the after-party on an early Sunday morning. The rest of the crew had called it a night after the wedding reception had ended over two hours ago, but Danny still had some party in him so he went out alone. The putrid smell of vomit smothered his nostrils. He stumbled past an obviously drunken man as he made his way to his car. He burped, the stale taste of beer mixed with liver and onions painted his taste palette staring into the shiny car window, startled Danny. The reflection showed a pale-faced drunk with vomit covering his face and neck staring at the back of his head. Danny instantly swung around facing the man who was now so close that he could not only smell the man's breath but could also feel it on his face. Danny took a step back leaning on his car coming by the stench. The man remained silent as he stood his ground in a dominant fashion, boxing Danny between himself and the car. Danny stared into his deep blue eyes as flashes of anger hit Danny just as unexpectedly as the man had appeared. Caution mixed with a tinge of fear struck Danny, bringing him back to his right mind and losing his alcohol high, but it was too late. The man had gotten the drop on him. Danny's eyes darted down toward the stranger's hands. He noticed the man clutching a long-barreled revolver. Danny grabbed the barrel of the gun and the two began to struggle. The assailant started squeezing. Four shots rang out before Danny stopped wrestling with the man and dropped down on the side of his car bleeding. The man fired the remaining two shots into Danny's chest, bent down, and tried to wedge Danny's bloody frame between the curb and his car. Danny stared, speechless and wide-eyed as the man dropped the gun into his coat pocket, he quickly scanned up and down the block before walking away.

* * *

Short Stack knew he was wrong to stay out all night, but he didn't feel like dealing with Monique and her constant bickering and crying. Ever since they had left the reception she had been a constant headache for no apparent reason. He had made it a point to try to make it right with her and he had bent over backwards trying to make her happy, but nothing worked. So he dropped her off at home and went to spend the night over at Samantha's. He surprised himself sometimes, as fine as she was he still refused to go there with her. Samantha was nice enough, but he still saw her as more like a little cousin than anything else. So although she offered her bed again, he slept on the couch. She went to bed pouting but he was oblivious to her feelings. Just as he began to doze off a loud banging on the door made him jump to his feet. Samantha rushed into the living room cursing and covering herself with her robe.

"Who is it?" she yelled through the door as she turned on the living room light.

"It's Rodney." the voice yelled back. Samantha unlocked the door. Rodney rushed in and looked toward Short Stack. Samantha rolled her eyes as she closed the door and headed back toward her bedroom.

"I knew you were here." Rodney blurted out ignoring Samantha's gesture.

"What's up? What's going on?" Short Stack asked with an annoyed look across his face.

"Let's go, man. Danny is in the hospital. He got hit with a bunch of leads about an hour ago. They don't know if he gonna make it. Phil-Fine and your brother are already at the hospital."

Samantha stopped and turned back towards Rodney Pipe staring wide-eyed as Short Stack jumped from the sofa he was laying on snatching his trousers from the floor and sliding them on.

"What the fuck man?" Short Stack mumbled under his breath as he slid both shoes on at the same time. Rodney Pipe remained silent, the two men rushed out of the apartment leaving the door open. Samantha closed the door and turned out the lights.

* * *

Sitting in a parked car with the engine running in front of Giovanni's, a neighborhood diner on the North Side, the man who had just gunned Danny down sat bare chested wiping his face and neck with his shirt. He rolled down his window and dropped his shirt on the ground. The streets were quiet except for a junkie passing by here and there. The rest of the neighborhood was gone to bed. Although he could've moved out a long time ago, he remained in the old neighborhood. He thought, Hell, he earned his living here, so why not live here? Besides, he loved the old neighborhood and it loved him back. He lit a cigarette as a dark-colored Sedan pulled up across the street and parked. A short, stocky figure approached his car, walked around to the passenger side, and got in.

"You just had to do it, didn't you?"

"Don't start breaking my balls, Ira."

"I told you it's a process to this thing. We don't go off half-cocked just shooting up shit like some trigger-happy moolies."

"It's over with now, Ira. So are we going to continue with this thing or are you gonna keep bitching at me like I'm a teenage kid who just stole your car for a joy ride?" Ira waived his hands as he spoke, his pointer finger constantly brushing the tip of the lone gunman's nose. He was annoyed by the disrespectful gesture but what could he do? Not only was Ira his uncle he also was a boss.

"You fucking kids never listen. Don't you move on those Trenton boys again until I say so you hear me?"

The man sat silent as he took a long hard draw from his cigarette. "Am I fucking talking to myself, kid?"

"I hear you, Ira."

Ira kissed the young man on the cheek. "Don't fucking play with me, kid. Go home, get cleaned up, get some rest, and keep your nose clean. Come see me in a few days, Charlie. I might have some work for you."

Ira got out of the car, walked across the street, climbed into his car, and then pulled off. The man sat watching as his thoughts raced. He didn't give a damn about the Trentons or what his uncle thought was best. Ira was old and he had had his turn at things. Taking over Trenton's operation was the last thing on the young man's mind. It would be a bonus, but wiping them and their entire crew out was his main priority.

* * *

Short Stack rushed into the hospital visiting room. The first person he saw was Monique. "Fuck!" He thought to himself. She was the last person he wanted to see right now. He acknowledged her by kissing her on the cheek.

"You alright?"

Monique nodded yes. Short Stack turned and glanced around the room. Phil-Fine stood with his back to him talking on the phone. Blue Ball held Apricot as she cried. Lil-Larry sat alone in a corner of the waiting room reading a magazine. He was surprised to see him and thought it was strange that he was there, but brushed it off. Short Stack left Monique as he re-joined Rodney Pipe.

"So don't nobody know shit?" Short Stack said.

Rodney Pipe stuck his hands in his pants pocket and leaned against the wall. "I ain't heard nothing yet," he answered.

"Somebody knows something, somebody always knows something."

"Don't you think I know that shit, man? The streets are always talking. We'll find out."

Phil-Fine hung up the phone and joined the two men. "That was Uncle Jermaine out in Cali. He said he gonna sneak back into town as soon as he can. He still waiting on Carlin to sort this shit out with him and the IRS, but to keep him posted about Danny's health status until he can get home," he said.

"So if ain't nobody seen shit, how y'all find out he was here?" Short Stack asked.

Phil-Fine answered, "The old man who runs the after-hours joint Danny was at came out to close up this morning and found him lying next to his car. He called the ambulance then called Randy."

Blue Ball joined the men and hugged his little brother. "You alright, man?"

Short Stack shrugged his shoulders. "Shit, I'm fine, just want some answers."

Randy came into the visiting area joined by a doctor. The doctor's face held a stern but sympathetic look as he flipped through the pages attached to the clipboard. He looked up from the clipboard and spoke towards Phil-Fine. "Mr.

Trenton was hit in several vital organs and a lot of his tissue muscles were damaged. Although he will be confined to a wheelchair for a while, with exercise and rehabilitation it will be possible for him to walk again."

Phil-Fine smiled. The doctor continued. "But I am sad to say that he will be forced to wear a bag for the rest of his life."

"What does that mean, doc?" Rodney Pipe asked.

Phil-Fine grimaced at Rodney Pipe as if he had asked a stupid question. He spoke down to Rodney Pipe out of anger, "That means my brother gonna have to wear a shit bag for the rest of his life."

Rodney Pipe overlooked Phil-Fine speaking directly toward the doctor. "I heard of that before Doc knew an old man from Louisiana who had an intertube hooked up with perfume and shit in it to cover the smell."

The doctor folded his arms biting into his bottom lip. "That's not unheard of unfortunately modern medicine hasn't come up with anything to combat this problem so folk in this predicament have to do what they deem necessary. I'll put you, folks, in touch with someone who can help."

Apricot, who had now joined the men asked, "When will he be well enough to talk?"

The doctor placed a gentle hand on Apricot's shoulder. "He just came out of surgery. He should be coherent sometime tomorrow night, but I still suggest you keep visits down to a minimum for at least seventy-two hours."

"Thank you, doctor," Phil-Fine said. The doctor and Apricot both walked away talking.

Blue Ball hugged his brother again and said good night to the men before leaving.

Rodney Pipe looked down at his feet and then exhaled. He gazed at the group of men in the room with wrinkled brows and a frown. He said, "So what now? I mean, there's no doubt we gonna find these assholes who were behind this. Had to be some dumb kid trying to make a name for himself or a wild cowboy looking for a come-up, but what about the crew? With Jermaine on the run, and Danny out of commission for a while, who gonna run shit?"

"Phil-Fine gonna have to run shit for a while. Look, you gonna have to take a back seat to that honeymoon til' your brother get well or Jermaine get home, whichever first," Short Stack said as a matter of fact.

Phil-Fine tried to hide his expression of disapproval, but all of the men read it across his face.

Randy intervened. "Fuck it, I got it for a little while until shit gets smoothed out."

"Aw hell naw," Short Stack yelled out.

"What? I can handle it," Randy said, defending himself.

"No the fuck you can't, you are not diplomatic enough to run shit. Me, you, or Rodney Pipe, we all got our points, but be honest. We are all quicker to go to the guns than this kid here and that's what we need to keep this ship from going under. It's more to this than street shit."

Randy scowled at Short Stack. He didn't appreciate him talking to him this way.

"We all know Phil-Fine ain't cut out for this. Shit, he doesn't even want this. You heard him last night."

"Want it or not, I got it. My daddy and my uncle Jermaine built this shit, and I ain't about to let it go all to hell the first time a crisis comes up. I'm making sure my daddy doesn't end up coming home to a crumbled empire."

Although Randy was pissed, he was loyal. He respected the Trenton's and what they stood for. "You got my support brother," he said as he placed a firm grip on the back of Phil-Fine's neck.

"Good, 'cause while I figure shit out I need you to stick close to me."

* * *

MUSCLE GAME

Boy- Boy relished the life, and spent every waking moment immersed in it. He had ambitions of someday owning his own bank and becoming a member of the Big Six. The right side of his facial skin was gone where he had been burnt the year before, leaving a lifetime scar of pink flesh. He rode down 94th street just after leaving a meeting about a job that paid very well. A hit. The most he had ever been paid. Almost triple the going rate, but that wasn't the thing that shocked him. What had his mind going was the person who *hired* him!

* * *

A Spoonful was sitting in the kitchen reading a local newspaper when she heard the front door open and then close. She looked up at the clock. It is eleven thirty in the afternoon too early for Lil-Percy to be home from school. She was going give that boy a piece of her mind, he already had gotten jumped on and beat to a pulp if he had his ass in school that would'nt have happened.

She yelled out, "Boy, what you doing home so early?"

No one answered. She stormed into the living room and stopped in her tracks. "Bird!"

Bird stood in the middle of the room wearing a confident and triumphant smile. "What? Ten years ain't long enough?" He let out a sexy laugh.

She screamed a joyous scream and jumped into Bird's arms, kissing his face and squeezing him tight.

"When you get out?" She screeched in an anxious voice.

"They let me out a few hours ago." He said as he lifted her from her feet as he hugged her back, twirling her about the room and falling on top of her onto the sofa.

"You just don't know, *Mama missed you so much!* What do you want, baby? You can get whatever you want?"

"Whatever I want?" A Spoonful looked at Bird with flirting eyes.

"Whatever!"

"Well, it is something I ain't tasted in about ten years."

A Spoonful licked her lips.

"You ain't got to tell me, Daddy. I already know. You just sit down on the couch and relax."

Bird took a seat on the couch and removed his shirt.

A Spoonful yelled from the kitchen. "You ready for it, Daddy?"

"Hell yeah!" Bird yelled, his voice filled with anticipation.

A Spoonful unbuttoned the top three buttons of her blouse, as she spoke from the kitchen. "Well, here it comes." She entered the living room carrying two glasses of beer and sat on Bird's lap.

"See, that's why I love you. You always know what daddy needs."

A Spoonful handed one of the glasses to Bird. "To new beginnings!"

* * *

In all his life the streets had never been as quiet as they had been the past three weeks. Phil-Fine couldn't understand it; they utilized all of their resources. They put out a fifty-thousand-dollar reward for any information given. They had people on every corner and boulevard, questioning every major and minor player in the game, gangsters and conmen, prostitutes and junkies. They talked with their men in the police department; no one was coming up off any information. Phil-Fine feared that so much time passed while he was at the helm, he made the crew look weak. He pulled up in front of his brother's home and parked. Although he had been home for almost two weeks, Phil-Fine had been avoiding him. He didn't think he had the stomach to see his brother in the condition he was in. Phil-Fine was becoming a little more comfortable with running things. It became a little more natural day by day. Uncle Jermaine still hadn't returned.

He hired a few extra boys for security, and sent Short Stack and Rodney Pipe to East Chicago to expand the numbers thing and get rid of some of the pounds Danny had flown in from Jamaica. Randy still stuck to him like glue. It was cool in the beginning because he felt like he might need the advice and Randy would be a good crutch to lean on when shit got too hectic. But he felt as if he was coming into his own and needed Randy less and less. But the more he expressed that, the more Randy clung on to him. Randy told Phil-Fine that it was his responsibility to keep him safe. Danny had told him to and that's what he would do until that bastard who put that hit out on Danny was taken care of.

Phil-Fine turned off the engine and got out of the car. He walked up the winding stairs to the house. Armed men with shotguns stood on opposite sides of the yard guarding the house. They both nodded at Phil-Fine. He twisted the doorknob of the front door and pushed it open. Apricot and Danny were arguing as Killer Danny's rottweiler rushed toward the door barking.

"Shut yo ass up!" Phil-Fine commanded as he closed the door and walked into the living room. Killer stopped barking, lowering his head and following Phil-Fine into the living room.

"What the hell is going on? Y'all making so much noise y'all ain't even hear me coming in."

Apricot shot Danny a nasty glare before walking over to Phil-Fine and giving him a warm hug and kiss on the cheek.

"Yuh know wha...mi left ya so an' any how mi hear she you ah trouble him ah pure hell mi ah go bring pon fi yuh rasscclot.

"Go head, sis. I got him."

Apricot leans over and kisses Danny on the lips then kisses Phil-Fine on the cheek.

"Alright babes, yuh done know."

"Love you, too sis. Phil-Fine says as he kisses her back on the cheek."

"Uno behaves." She exited the house followed by two bodyguards.

Phil-Fine checked the time on his watch before removing the handkerchief from his suit jacket and brushing the dust from the toes of his beige leather shoes. "What the hell is your problem, Danny?"

Danny spun around in his wheelchair and rolled into the kitchen ignoring the question. Phil-Fine followed.

"We ain't that far gone that you don't respect me enough to answer me when I ask you a question, are we?"

Danny turned back toward Phil-Fine. "Don't come to me with that bullshit. It's bad enough I'm stuck in this chair for the time being, but you make matters worse with this punk ass kid following me around all the time."

"We not talking about this again. He came highly recommended and you know him. He's like family. He's Aunt Tania's little cousin."

"Come on, Phil. Shit, he is only sixteen. I got shoes older than his ass!"

"When you ran shit I did what you said. Now it's your turn to learn some humility and let people take care of you. You don't know what's best all the time and I ain't discussing this shit no more. Scripture stays, the other security staff stays, and I know I'm crossing the line getting in your personal shit with you and your old lady. But you my big brother and I love you; I love her too, so take it easy on her a little bit, okay?"

Danny spun his chair in circles on two wheels in a playful manner. "Yeah, you are taking it too far. Don't interfere in how I run my household."

"I ain't trying to. I know Apricot is a tough-ass broad. She got to be with you. You a mutha fucka. I can just imagine how you are since you are in that chair. But I'm telling you, brah, it's shit you too close to see, so I'm here to open your eyes."

Danny rolled over to the refrigerator and removed a jug of freshly squeezed orange juice.

"You want some?"

"Yeah," Phil-Fine said as he removed two glasses from the upper cabinet and set them on the kitchen counter. Danny poured the juice.

"Shit like what, Phil?"

"Shit like she calls me crying, and talks to Sandra about how you won't touch her at night, and no matter what she does, you're never happy."

"That's bullshit! She ain't said shit to me about none of this."

Danny knew it was true. He hadn't touched her since he came home, even though they both knew that he was still able to perform sexually. Although his legs were temporarily paralyzed, his penis still got hard. The doctor told both him and Apricot that having sex was not only okay but it was encouraged. Danny still felt like less of a man, not having use of his legs and would verbally take it out on Apricot.

Phil-Fine continued, "She probably never will. She loves you man and you will always be her man. Think about it: She hasn't changed that much to accommodate your situation. She doesn't baby you or have people doing everything around here for you. You don't know it, but a couple of the boys done came to me complaining 'bout how she cursed them out for doing too much for you around here. She doesn't want to enable you. She knows you are a strong man and that you can handle anything. That's no doubt."

"Your point is?"

"My point, muh fucka is that she wants you to continue to acknowledge her as your woman. We both know just like men, women have needs too. That's all I got to say."

Danny knew his brother was right he downed the rest of his juice and rolled towards the front door. "So where is Scripture?" Danny asked.

"I told him to meet us in a few hours over at the Palm Inn. I wanted to spend a few hours with my big brother. I'm gonna take you to your physical therapist."

Danny snatched the front door open. He stared Phil-Fine in his eyes. "How come you never came to see me in the hospital? And this is your first time coming to see me and I've been home almost a month?"

Phil-Fine paused. He signaled for the two-armed guards. They rushed over and carried Danny down the stairs in his wheelchair to Phil-Fine's car. Phil-Fine followed behind as he opened the car door, picked his brother up, and placed him in the passenger seat. He closed the door turning his face from his brother to avoid eye contact, he was ashamed. "I'm here now, big brother, I'm here now."

* * *

Three weeks had gone past since the meeting with Ira in front of Giovanni's and Ira still hadn't made a move. What the fuck was he waiting on? Either Ira was gonna do something, or he wasn't. He felt like too much time was going by. The time to strike was now and he had to take things into his own hands once again. This time he would take it up a notch. He headed toward the old neighborhood to meet with Freddy Fingers, an old timer, He felt he had a better chance of getting Freddy to see eye to eye with him than he could Ira.

* * *

It was lights out at the Terre Haute Federal Penitentiary. Phil-Good lay awake staring at the ceiling. He could not sleep. Thoughts of the Palm Inn, his kids, and his old school partners filled his mind. He tried not to let his mind slip into a depressive mode thinking about Danny. He hated restless nights. He knew he would be up all night and tired as hell the next day. Well, he did have another reason to be wide-eyed. It was the third Thursday of the month. Every third Thursday of the month in the middle of the night he received a visitor.

He heard the lock outside his door unlock then the sound of the door creaking open. He sat up in his bed. His heart raced as he stared into the dark the scent of perfume reached him before the sexy silhouette did. A dark figure wearing a guard uniform entered and the door closed. Phil-Good stood and took the person into his arms and began kissing and groping in an animal-like fashion. He unbuttoned the uniform's top. Perfect round breasts popped out of the shirt. Phil-Good took the breast into his mouth, a sensual gasp escaped from her. He picked the small woman up off her feet, she wrapped both legs around him as she buried her face in his neck taking all of his scent in as she sucked and kissed his neck. Phil-Good took his time loving the woman in a passionate fashion, but not too much time. Tossing her on the bed and pouncing on top of her and grabbing he chin she threw her head back as Phil-Good ran his tongue down her neck he ripped the shirt open the buttons popped off hitting the walls in all directions she respired in desperation. He had to have her gone before the morning count, they sexed passionately and violently three times, four hours later she got dressed and hurried from the room. It was costing him a pretty penny for these extra amenities, but it was worth it. *Pussy* was worth more than money where he was now.

***

Royal Talker pulled up in front of his home and parked his car. Getting out and locking the door, he waved to the little boys riding their bikes in the streets. Life was good, a long way from the life he once lived, he traded in his guns for a briefcase. He had everything to live for a beautiful wife, a great career, and no longer had to look over his shoulders when he walked the streets. Stepping up the stairs to the front door of the duplex he lived in. Reaching for the doorknob he paused, turning back towards the car he had forgotten a bouquet of flowers he'd bought for his wife on the front seat he thought of running back to the car to get them but turned back towards the house he'd come back out after he ran in to use the restroom. Placing the key into the lock and turning he gripped the doorknob and turned, pushing the door open an explosion-blast swept Royal off the stairs and dropped him into the street!

***

Blue Ball was coming out of a neighborhood bar on 46th and Wabash when he was walking to his car. A man in his fifties rushed past looking as if the devil himself was on his heels. Blue Ball had seen that look in men's eyes before. He played the background, got into his car and followed the man for about half a block, and then sped ahead and threw his passenger door open.

"Get in and lay on the floor!"

The stranger kept walking looking at Blue Ball out the corner of his eye. Blue Ball continued driving next to the man waving his arm anxiously at the man.

"Hey you, I know you hear me talking to you. Get in man!" The man looked up at Blue Ball with a befuddled expression plastered across his face; hesitantly he jumped in and slammed the door closed. Blue Ball pulled up to a red light as three police cars with their sirens roaring sped past.

Looking into the rearview mirror Blue Ball continued driving at a slow pace. "They for you?"

"Like you wouldn't believe!"

***

The chit-chat with Freddy Fingers went about as well as he had expected. The old man said he would serve as consigliere, but he would not get involved. Although they weren't officially mob-connected, they still had rules to follow. There was a street hierarchy to this thing that could potentially mess up a lot of money the big bosses had going and spark a potential war. He couldn't afford to have his name mixed up in this thing should it backfire. It was Freddy's idea to put the hit on Royal. Although he was only connected to the Kings and the rackets through association, Freddy still thought that taking him out would serve as a nice message that they weren't going away and anyone at any time could end up suspect to a dirt nap.

* * *

Pastor Barry sat alone in his hotel room he rented over on 17th and Langley drank himself into a stupor. His thoughts were filled with the things he had done in his younger years and he knew God was going to judge him for them. He hadn't thought about the murders for years, but seeing Paul Anthony made them all come flooding back. As he was preparing to open another bottle, a loud banging startled him. He dropped the bottle. It shattered. He clutched a handgun and yanked the door open. Blue Ball stood on the other side of the door. His mouth opened in shock from not only seeing the Pastor drunk on his feet but also gripping a gun.

"Everything all right Pastor?" Blue Ball asked, looking around suspiciously.

The Pastor too drunk to feel embarrassed left the door open. Blue Ball entered and closed the door behind himself. Pastor Barry threw the gun on the bed and flopped down on the bed. Blue Ball pulled the chair from the desk and sat down.

"I'm fine, I guess you could say I'm paranoid. Been having nightmares. They seem so real."

"Maybe you got some stuff on your mind you need to talk about."

"No, don't worry about me, son. I'll be fine. What can I do for you?"

"I'm giving up the rackets."

"I heard. Good, good for you."

"I have a question, Pastor."

"Shoot."

"Does God accept anyone to do his work? I mean, I've done some horrible things in my life, including taking lives."

"Not tonight, son I'm the wrong person to ask." The Pastor stood and threw his arms around Blue Ball in a tight hug laughing.

Blue Ball brows narrowed. He didn't want to push the issue seeing the condition Pastor Barry was in. He would ask another time when the pastor was sober.

"I feel good about myself, Pastor."

"Oh yeah, why is that?"

"I did a good deed. At least I think it was good." Blue Ball shrugged.

"You don't know for sure?" Pastor Barry asked as he removed a flask from his pocket unscrewed the cap and placed it to his lips.

"You see earlier today this guy was trying to get away, from who I don't know. I just know he needed help so I pulled over and let him jump in. Just in time, too. The police rolled past not even seconds after he got in."

"You could look at it in either fashion. One, you could've helped an innocent man get away from crooked cops. Or two, helped a child molester or rapist evade capture. You have to be careful with the deeds you choose to pursue. They say you can't save everybody for a reason."

* * *

Bird, dressed in a dirty white T-shirt, blue jean overalls, and steel-toed work boots, loaded a pick-up truck with tools. He turned to Mr. Nelson, the neighborhood-roofing contractor. He'd promised A Spoonful that he would do nothing but honest work. So here he was living a square's life and doing square's work. But as long as his woman was happy, that was all he really cared about.

"We're finally done, huh?" Bird asked Mr. Nelson.

"Hell yeah."

"Here go the best part. This what I have been waiting all week for." Mr. Nelson reached into his pocket and pulled out some money. He counted it and handed the bills to Bird.

Bird took the money and began counting it. His face twisted, his eyes squinted, and his lips clenched. "Man, it's been damn near eleven years since I done held paper money in my hands."

"Yeah I know, but you spend it quicker than it takes to get it."

"Right, right, but uh, Mr. Nelson, I think you made a mistake. I know I only worked a week, but this is barely half of what I'm supposed to be paid for the amount of work I did."

"Yeah, I know. The guy ain't give me all the money. He said we got to wait until Monday. Don't worry about it, you gonna get paid and I got some more jobs lined up. You going be all right."

Bird's face was a blanket of anger. He got right in Mr. Nelson's face. When he spoke, spit was splattering on his face.

"I'm going be all right ... I'm going be all right? *I just did ten years in the federal penitentiary, man. I'll fuck you up if you don't get me the rest of my money. Not now, but right now!*"

Mr. Nelson tried not to show any fear. "Calm down, you'll be paid."

Bird yelled, "*You mutha fucking right I'm gonna be paid!*"

"Just not today. My hands are tied. Listen, none of the other guys are getting all their pay either."

"You think I give a fuck *what the other guys* get . . . I'm talking 'bout me and mines. Now get me the rest of my money before I get violated back for beating the shit out of you 'bout my money!"

Mr. Nelson reached into his pocket, pulled out the money, counted out some, and handed it to Bird.

"Look, we can't be having this shit on the job site. What can I expect though from niggas like you. This gonna be your last job working for me."

"That's cool. Long as I'm paid what I'm owed. I ain't got to never work for your old weasel ass no more."

Bird climbed onto the back of the pick-up truck and sat down.

Mr. Nelson rushed towards the truck slamming his hands on the side of the truck. "What are you doing?"

"Shit, I'm waiting on you to take me home. I ain't walk here, muh fucka."

Bird leaned back against the truck and pulled his hat down over his face. Mr. Nelson didn't want to take him home he had just fired him. He didn't want to fight him either that surely would be the result of telling him to get off his truck and get home the best way he could. So Mr. Nelson huffed and grunted but he never uttered a word he climbed into the truck slammed the door closed and throwing the truck into drive jerked off into traffic.

Within a half-hour, he was hopping out the back of the truck and trekking up the stairs of the duplex. He put in his key and turned the lock. Upon entering, he kicked off his boots, took off his dirty shirt, and dropped it on the floor next to his boots. He laid his tool bag on top.

A Spoonful rose from the couch and greeted her man with a hug and a kiss. "How was work, baby?" she asked, following behind him hugging his waist. He walked over to the living room window and stared out at the desolate streets. The sun was setting and the impoverished ghetto he had called home all his life almost looked serene.

"Get dressed, we stepping out."

A Spoonful stepped behind her man wrapping her arms around him and laying her head on his back. "Out? We can't afford to go out besides ..."

"I got this now. Gone on and get pretty for me. We stepping out."

"What about Lil Percy?"

"He old enough to fend for self. This is about you and me tonight. Lay something out for me to wear, too." Bird knew what had to be done no need to dwell on it, so he figured he might as well treat his baby out to a night on the town when things he had in mind unfolded she definitely would be upset.

* * *

Pastor Barry rolled out of bed yawned and stretched his legs, glancing down at his pistol sitting on the nightstand near the bed picking it up he opened the barrel spun it closed it then walked into the bathroom and closed the door.

* * *

Paul Anthony wore his hair in dreadlocks and had a full silver-colored beard. He rode down 24th and West Lake Street in the used Ford he had bought. The vehicle handled well. He knew what he had to do, but it didn't sit well with him. He thought to himself, "*I'm too old for this shit!*" Paul Anthony thought about letting it slide, but letting it slide was the reason he had lost almost a hundred and fifty pounds. His conscience was fucking with him. His brothers were haunting him in his sleep. He knew the man who had killed them was still walking around carefree and he didn't do a thing about it. He got word he was in Chicago. It wasn't easy 'cause he had changed his name and became a preacher. If a man was determined enough, he could find whatever it is he was looking for. Paul Anthony knew he would have to do this right the first time. He would not get a second chance. Going back to prison was not an option.

He pulled the car around to the back of the building and parked. Walked into the hotel up the stairs and down the hall sweat ran through his palm as he grappled the butt of the pistol. With each step he took he felt his heart pound eyeballing the hall he crept towards his prey. Stopping at the last door at the end of the hall, placing his ear to the door he listened then stepped back and kicked the door open. The door flung open he rushed in, eyes darting around the room he scrambled across the room yanking the closet door open, nothing there tip-toeing towards the bathroom he clutched the doorknob and slowly pushed the door open wide-eyed brandishing the pistol. His heart skipped a beat to find Pastor Barry standing there with his pistol trained on him. The barrel of the gun blinded his eyesight; he slowly stepped back into the room Pastor Barry haltingly followed him out of the bathroom. Pastor Barry said, "You didn't go for the Pastor thing, huh?"

Paul Anthony waived the gun nonchalantly as he spoke. "Yeah, I knew you were a real Pastor, but that doesn't change what you did and what I got to do."

"Yeah, I suppose not." Pastor Barry says as he rocked from side to side nervously.

"I mean, we have history together and this is a chapter that has to come to an end." Paul Anthony said pointing the gun in the Pastor's face as sweat ran down his nose.

"I agree, but we write our own stories. We don't have to end it like this, not in *this* way!"

"A man got to live with himself."

Pastor Barry steps towards Paul Anthony freezing in his tracks as Paul Anthony cocks back the hammer on the pistol.

"How did you find me? I always thought you would die in prison!" Pastor Barry asked as he felt his palms getting damp with perspiration.

"I almost did, but God blessed me with an opportunity and I took it. Me and a couple of the other boys busted out. One got killed by a guard, shot in the back. One got caught two days ago I read in the paper, and the other I don't know where his ass at. Don't too much care. But you know what the funny thing is?"

"No what's that?"

"I almost didn't make this little meeting. I was coming out of a bar the other day and a bounty hunter comes in showing my picture. I duck out the back of the place trying not to cause attention to myself cause I know the police are coming and just when I knew I was caught, a car pulls over and gives me a ride. That's when I *knew* it was meant for me to kill you."

"That's not the sign I would've got from it."

"Yeah, well me and you two different people."

"I suppose we are, or maybe we're more alike than you know."

"Sorry Pastor!"

"Me too!"

Pastor Barry and Paul Anthony both raised their guns at the same time and pulled the trigger. However, Pastor Barry was a hair quicker than Paul. When he pulled the trigger the click, click, click sound of empty barrels were heard right before the slugs from Paul Anthony's gun tore into his chest like a knife into a wet paper bag.

Pastor Barry smiled. "Beat you!" He slumped over on the side of the bed and died.

Paul Anthony became infuriated. He felt cheated. The feelings he felt of being a coward or an unloyal brother he thought would alleviate by avenging his brothers' deaths intensified. He jumped up and down, cursing Pastor Barry and his mother for having him. He walked over to the dead man's body and opened his hand. Bullets from the pastor's gun fell to the floor.

* * *

Phil-Good, Needles, and Piranha roam the prison yard speaking in whispered tones.

Phil-Good felt Needles breath on his neck as he spoke into his ear, "I got some shit I need to lay on you." Needles paused to check for Phil-Good's body action.

Phil-Good turned towards Needles and looked into his eyes as if he was trying to read into his soul. "Go ahead, young blood."

"Well, first off I got word that this whole thing has been unofficially orchestrated by a young white boy from out the Madiassa camp."

Phil-Good's face was enveloped in confusion. "Madiassa camp? Who do they go through in here? I know it wasn't Der Orden. The Corelli's?"

"Yeah, you know it. They got a little more pull in La Cosa Nostra than the Madiassa family. Not much ... but more all the same. I figure they knew fucking with you straight on would bring heat in the streets off your name alone and heat from us in here. Them mutha fuckas know you got ties with us. That's why they got Der Orden involved."

"I'll give the Corelli's a pass this time. But get word to the boy in charge of their camp to call off the dogs he sent at me and I won't send them killers at what he holds close to his heart."

"I thought you might say that, so I took the initiative to add a little incentive to force the Corelli's to make a favorable decision."

"I don't even want to know."

Piranha smirked.

***

Paul Anthony unlocked the door to his room. He had been renting from an elderly couple who ran a boarding house. He took off his jacket, threw it across the bed, and threw the gun he removed from his gun holster on the dresser. Kicking off his shoes, he removed the cap from the bottle of whiskey and poured himself a drink. He was anxious to get out of Chicago. It was a two-hour ride to Detroit, next, he would get over the border to Canada. He had made it this far on the run and did not intend to go back. He walked across the hall to the bathroom and turned on the water in the tub. He had planned to take a bath, change, and eat a hot meal before he hit the road. He traded in his car for another just to be cautious. As he walked back across the hall to his room to get his robe, he ran into a young man in the hall. Although the kid didn't strike him as a threat, it was still something about him that Paul Anthony couldn't put his finger on. He figured he would be cordial and speak, but still give the young blood some distance. He grabbed his robe and dashed back to the bathroom. Closing the door, he stripped out of his clothing and climbed into the steaming hot water.

He laid back against the tub, took a deep breath, sighed, and then closed his eyes. He sank down into the steaming hot water. Quickly emerging and wiping the water from his face, the young man from across the hall stood over him pointing a gun.

Blinking his eyes quickly, he stuttered in a hushed tone, "I, I, I, don't have any money, son none worth stealing anyway."

The man standing over him didn't say a word. He pulled the trigger twice cutting into Paul Anthony's chest, turning the water red with Paul's blood. Still calm and unnerved, he watched the body jerk, violently splashing water to the floor, and then stopped moving. He looked into the mirror checking his burnt, scarred face for blood splatter. The reflection in the mirror is Boy-Boy. This was his first solo hit and his most paid one, too. He always included Lil Larry in on every dollar he made, just an unwritten thing they had amongst themselves. But they had to cut the cord sooner or later. Besides Pastor Barry wanted the hit as quiet as possible since he was the client. So Boy-Boy respected his wishes and kept Lil Larry out of the loop.

* * *

Scripture walked into the mental ward of the hospital in the North Suburb of Chicago. Dressed in an all-white orderly uniform pushing a wheelchair and carrying a clipboard, he went unnoticed. He entered the first room in the hall closed and locked the door he placed the clipboard on the dresser. Stepping cautiously across the room he surveyed the terrain. It was as expected the room held a damp musty odor, the type of smell that some old folks just seem to exude from their flesh. In the corner of the room sat a bed with an elderly white man lying asleep. Scripture moved towards the bed and stood over the old man. Removing a roll of duct tape from the pocket of the orderly jacket he was wearing he stretched the tape out, the old man opened his eyes as he heard the noise, before he could react Scripture ripped a piece small enough to cover his mouth and placed it across his lips. Placing the tape back into his pocket he quickly picked the man up and sat him in the wheelchair first he taped both wrists to the arms of the chair then he taped both ankles to the legs. After placing the tape back into his pocket he reached into the opposite pocket and removed a surgeon's face mask and placed it across the old man's face to camouflage the duct tape covering his mouth. Walking back to the bed he jerked the blanket from the bed and covered the old man's frame to hide the fact that his arms and legs were bound. Picking up the clipboard from the dresser he opened the door and pushed the man from the room, down the hall, and out of the building. A truck sat out front the back popped open and Chuck the man who had beaten up Lil Percy hopped out helping Scripture pick up the wheelchair and place it into the truck they slammed the doors closed. Both men quickly scan the neighborhood to see if anyone was looking before climbing into the front of the truck and driving off.

***

Bird usually told his wife everything, but he didn't want to disappoint her. He had only been home a couple of days and already quit his job. He thought she would think he was up to his old tricks again. He was, but he honestly tried this time some people just weren't cut out for honest work those were his thoughts anyway. He knew she would never understand, and to make matters less complicated he would keep this under his hat besides what she didn't know wouldn't hurt her. So every morning he got dressed and went out job hunting. Four hours of the day he went job hunting. The other four hours he spent hustling at the pool hall, so he would have enough money at the end of the week as if he received a check. A Spoonful lay in bed as Bird got dressed. She stretches her legs wearing a schoolgirl smile, "You know you ain't supposed to be leaving the state, baby."

"Look, baby, don't worry. It's just a couple of hours to talk to this man about a job." He leaned down and kissed her.

"Love you, baby. See you later on tonight."

"Be careful, babe, and drive safe."

* * *

Jermaine whipped the Midnight Black colored Cadillac through the junk-yard parking lot laughing to himself as he watched the clouds of dust and loose stones kick up and hit the men gathered in a circle gambling. He got out of the car and joined the men. Danny sat in his wheelchair in the circle of thirty-odd men, watching the dogfight clutching a fist full of dollars. He didn't acknowledge his uncle right off. He continued watching the dogs fight as Phil-Fine and Randy hugged Jermaine and said hello. Jermaine walked over to where Danny sat and removed a wad of money. He signaled the guy who collected the bets to come over. The little Puerto Rican guy rushed over and took the money as Jermaine told him the dog he put his money on to win. Jermaine crouched down so that he was at eye level with Danny and continued watching the fight.

"How are you doing, nephew?"

"Alright, I guess, Unc."

"How Phil-Fine been doing?"

"Okay, I guess. He ain't lost control of the operations or no shit like that, but he ain't found out who the fucker was who put me in this chair either."

"Madiassa's boy."

"Ira?"

"He may be connected, but I mean literally Madiassa's boy. Johnny Hands son, Charlie Madiassa."

"Ain't nobody came to me about taking over the operations or no threats or nothing."

"He going off emotions. His pride hurt that his father was taken out of the equation and we still operating. He felt like we should have been taken care of by one of the families."

"What the fuck does he care? He was a kid, shit both of us was. We got to be around the same age. That shit was over twenty years ago."

"I'm just guessing about why he did it or should I say still doing it, 'cause you know that shit with Royal connected, don't you?"

"Yeah, I figured that. How you ain't been home, but maybe twenty-four hours and you figure more shit out than Phil do in weeks? "

"Carlin picked me up from the airport. He just came from seeing ya Daddy. He said his people on the inside pulled his coat to the happenings."

"Boy, daddy a trip. He locked down and still know more 'bout what's going on in the streets than we do."

"You know how it is. A lot of times them muh fuckas in there know what's gonna go down before the streets do."

"So we go at the Madiassa's hard and put this shit to bed before they come at us again?"

"Naw, we wait. Ya, pops got something going already. Let's see how that turns out first."

"You still on the run?"

"Hell yeah, had to see how you were doing that's the only reason I'm here."

"Y'all still ain't got ya tax shit right?"

"Carlin and my accountants working on shit now trying to account for all these millions I got. I thought I had my shit covered better ... my guy I had doing my books was an idiot. It's a mess."

"You'll figure it out. Aunt Tania come with you?"

"Yeah, she laid low. We rented a room and shit. Told her she can come to see everybody later tonight when more people were moving about in the streets so we can blend in. Look, son, I need you to keep a close eye on Phil. He gonna need you."

"As soon as I'm out of this chair, I got you. But right now I got Randy playing his shadow."

* * *

Corelli was next in line to be bumped up as a lieutenant in the Corelli crime family. He would've been moved up quicker had he not caught a bid for his participation in a string of highway hijackings. He and Yellow Boy were throwing names back and forth about who could've snatched Corelli's grandfather from his nursing home. First, they thought it was for a ransom, and then dismissed that because it had been twenty-four hours and still no phone call or ransom letter. Then, they thought it could've been a rival crew, but the Corelli's were on good standings with every family connected. Yellow Boy suggested an out-of-state crew or just dumb fucking luck. Maybe he wandered off and they were blowing it all out of proportion. But Corelli knew better. Corelli flopped down on the thin mattress and lay back against the wall. Both men sat in silence as they heard the old, rusty cart making its way down the tier and the voice of the inmate calling out names for mail call.

"Corelli!" he yelled out as he paused and handed the envelope to Yellow Boy.

"Anything in there for me, old timer?" Yellow Boy asked.

"That's all I got." He continued down the tier yelling names. Yellow Boy tossed the envelope on the mattress in front of Corelli. The front of the envelope had no stamp and no return address. It only read Corelli in big bold letters. Corelli flipped the envelope over and ripped it open. The envelope was empty except for ten little objects that looked like small pieces of strange plastic tainted with what looked like blood. He looked closer and poured the contents of the envelope into his hand.

"What the fu ..." Corelli said almost under his breath as he tossed the contents onto the floor.

"What is it, boss?" Yellow Boy asked, picking up the foreign objects.

Corelli leaped from the bed and rushed down the tier catching the mail delivery guy and slamming him against the cell bars.

"Where the fuck did you get that envelope, inmate?"

"Piranha threw it on my cart and told me to get it to you."

Corelli let the man go and rushed down the stairs and into the prison's weight room followed by Yellow Boy and three other soldiers from the Corelli family. They were stopped midway by two soldiers from The Bloody Feathers gang.

"What y'all want?" the short stocky one asked, directing his comment toward Corelli.

"We got an invitation from your boss. Now get him out here." Corelli conveyed as he anxiously bounced in place.

"You don't come down here bossing folks around, Corelli." The stocky one spewed out as he pushed one of Corelli's soldiers back.

"Fucking get him out here," Yellow Boy demanded.

Piranha paused from lifting weights, dropping the three- hundred-fifty-pound free-weight bar on the ground.

"Let 'em through," he demanded. He signaled for Needles to join them.

Corelli walked through as the two guards made room for him to pass. They let Yellow Boy pass through also but made the other soldiers wait at bay. Corelli glared at Needles. The four men stood in silence for several seconds. Yellow Boy spoke up.

"Where's that boot, Phil-Good?"

Needles smirked. "You get ya letter at mail call, Corelli?"

"He was a civilian for Christ's sake, a fucking old man. Why in the fuck would you do an old man in?" Corelli asked.

Yellow Boy threw the objects from his hand at Needles chest. They popped off his chest and hit the ground. He didn't flinch; his eyes turned into an icy glare. He spoke. "We ain't do the old man but don't think we won't. Those are just his fingernails. We had to get your attention, let you know we weren't fuckin' around. I heard it was some painful shit, having your fingernails popped off one by one. Put a leash on your wolves and Phil-Good guarantees the safe return of your grandfather. If not, shit, it only gets worse from here."

Corelli turned and walked away followed closely by Yellow-Boy. Yellow-Boy spoke in a hushed tone, "We not gonna let these moolies get away with this, are we?"

"Right now, yeah. What choice do I have? Got to get the old man back, alive. Get word to Der Orden and the Madiassa boy, but believe you me, when I say this shit ain't over."

***

Monique hated working the early shift. She yawned and greeted Lil Larry with a weak smile. As she walked into the restaurant prepared to start her workday, it dawned on her that she and Lil-Larry had been crossing paths a lot lately. The first time was the morning that Danny got shot. When she got the call and rushed out of the house to the hospital, she stopped at a gas station and he was there. She told him about Danny and he followed her to the hospital. The next time they saw each other, she was coming from her mother's house and he was sitting in a car. Lil Larry said he was waiting for a lady friend of his who lived on that block to come out. Now, here he was again leaving the restaurant. She didn't mention all the coincidences though.

"Good morning, Lil Larry. Up early, ain't we?"

"Yes, Ms. Monique. The early bird gets the worm."

Although she knew it wouldn't be right, she thought that she would do it anyway. She loved Short Stack to death, but she was lonely and hurt. He had been gone for weeks now and hadn't once asked her to come down and visit him or anything.

"Larry, I need a favor." She asked as she struck a seductive pose and twirled her finger through her hair.

"Yeah? Anything for Short Stack."

"Hmph, Short Stack? I think it would be wise if neither of us mentioned this to Short Stack."

A devious smile spread across his face.

"It's just dinner, so you can get that goofy-looking smirk off your face. I just want some company. If you can't handle that, let me know now," she said staring into his eyes hoping he still agreed to come.

Lil-Larry heard what she said, but in his mind, it would happen eventually. Maybe not tonight, but soon he would be in her bed and next in her heart.

"No problem, dinner is cool."

Monique knew he thought he had a chance at more, but that was his hang-up. All she could do was be upfront and honest. She had no intentions of cheating on Short Stack. If he built up his expectations for a disappointing letdown, that was on him.

"Okay, I get off at three. Give me a few hours to get home, clean up and cook. Stop by at about eight or so."

"Sounds good, see you at eight." Then out the door, he went.

* * *

Corelli did everything he could to hold back his emotions. He was pissed, but he had to remain calm. Ira was doing him a favor he didn't even have to get involved, Corelli needed Ira so the least he could do was hold his tongue and try not to disrespect the man. Ira sat across from Corelli in the visiting room of the Terre Haute Penitentiary.

"Thank you for coming out to see me. I hate to get you involved in this, but I saw no other way around it."

Ira leaned back in his seat and folded his arms. "What is it, kid?" He gestured with his hands in an inpatient manner.

"You know your nephew came to me for a favor, and my family and your family go so far back, who am I to say no?"

"I'm listening."

"Okay, the thing is, this favor that I was asked to do didn't go the way we figured it should. So I got to step back. They snatched my grandfather from his fucking nursing home. Ripped off his fucking fingernails. I got no choice, I got to step back."

"Okay, what do you want me to do? Try to get the old man back or what?"

"No, I want you to get word to your crazy-ass nephew."

"Whoa, come on now. I understand you're upset about the old man, but that is my nephew."

"No disrespect, Ira, but this fucking guy practically spit in my face. I get word to him about what's going down; the fucker doesn't care. When my people get back to me they tell me he ain't say one way or the fucking other, if he's gonna step back or not."

"You fucking kids kill me. You're all the same. Run off and do shit without a care in the fucking world, and as soon as the shit blows up in your face, you run back to us for help. You fucking lucky I have a lot of love and respect for your grandfather. I learned a lot from the old guy. He's the only reason I'm going to have a talk with my nephew."

"Thank you, Ira. I owe you one."

"Tell me this kid. I had a talk with your brother, why is it that you didn't get the okay from him before you went through with this thing in the first place?"

"With all due respect, Ira. I appreciate the favor but don't ask me about the family. Corelli business is Corelli business."

"Well said, kid, well fucking said."

* * *

Bird stepped from the Greyhound bus with a cigarette resting between his lips. Looking up and down the desolate road he saw a truck quickly approaching. The truck pulled up and came to a stop, Bird snatched the door open and climbed into the passenger seat of the truck slamming the door closed as the truck jerked off into traffic. The driver was Chuck, the man he had to beat up his son for him.

"Welcome to the Windy City?" Choke exclaimed through clenched teeth.

"So what's the rundown on the gig?" Bird demanded as he blew out a gust of smoke.

"The hit on Phil-Good in the joint was by this small-time *Italian* clique. We got one of the wops granddaddy tied up in a basement. No ransom, just a guarantee that he gets returned alive if they pull back on trying to hit Phil and his people."

"Yeah, but how long is that shit gonna last? Soon as they get the old man back, they gonna come at Phil and them, full force."

"Yeah I know, but Phil's coming home real soon. I figured he was just trying to buy some time. He wants to handle the shit personally."

"Where do I come in at?"

Chuck continued steering with one arm reaching down he pulled his jacket he had laying on the seat in between the two of them onto the floor. Underneath the jacket was a Thompson machine gun.

"They smell a war coming on. They need more muscle. I ain't know if you needed work or not, but I know if I wanted anybody watching my ass when I'm thick in the trenches, it would be you."

Bird picked up the machine gun cocked it back and lay it on his lap.

"Shit a job is a job, um in."

* * *

Ira and Freddy Fingers stood in front of Giovanni's, the neighborhood deli eating pistachios and talking. Freddy Fingers spit a shell on the ground and popped another one into his mouth.

"What are we gonna do about this boy?" Ira bellowed,

"That's the thing, Ira, he ain't a boy no more."

"He ain't acting like a responsible man with all this cowboy shit. For what? He ain't earning a dime off it, he just doing it 'cause what? His feelings hurt? Get the fuck out of here with that."

"I hear you. I hear you, but it is what it is. We either clean it up or give the go-ahead for him to get whacked."

Ira irately shoved Freddy back, "What are you saying, you?"

Freddy knowing he had over spoken leerily stared back, "I'm just saying."

"Look, I had a talk with him. He says he understands the way it has to be, for right now anyway. I don't trust him though. You go with him. I need you to be his conscious; get the fucking old man back home safe. I gave my word to the Corelli's."

"No problem, boss. I'll guide the kid in the right direction."

* * *

Samantha sat in bed listening to her favorite Jazz album Sippie Wallace's "Devil Dance Blues" daydreaming about a life with Short Stack. She would be the perfect wife; he already treats her only son as if he was her own. It was only natural that they get married; he hadn't married Monique so it was more than obvious that he didn't really love her. All she needed was Short Stack to open his eyes and see; God men are so clueless sometimes she thought as a knock at the door revived her from her daydream. Not really in the mood for company she ignored the door. After a few seconds the knocking became louder it was obvious that the person at the door wasn't going away. She lay down on the bed throwing a pillow over her head, when she popped up it crossed her mind that it might be Short Stack at the door. Her heart skipped a beat she knew more so than not, that it wasn't Short Stack but she didn't want to take that chance she hadn't seen him in a while and was really beginning to miss him. Reluctantly she rose from her bed exited her bedroom and walked to the front door, standing on her tip-toes she looks through the peephole, her heart dropped to her disappointment its not Short Stack but her mother. It wasn't that she was unhappy to see her mother but she knew how it would go. It was always the same, her looking down on her for not being able to get and keep a man. She always stuck her nose where it didn't belong. She opened the door for her mother, who was an older version of her appearance-wise anyway. She was still pretty and often mistaken as Samantha's sister.

She walked in and closed the door.

"Where's my grandbaby?"

"He over to his daddy's."

"No company tonight? Where's that little short, *sexy* Muthafucka you always got over here?"

Samantha felt embarrassed. "Mama!"

"Girl, Mama what? You don't like men no more?"

Samantha closed the door moving across the living room, she drew the blinds back and peeked out the window avoiding her mother's eye contact. "No you know it's not that, but Short Stack and I are just friends."

"You got to be more aggressive, girl. Grab that little bull by his horns and rope him in."

Samantha laughed. "Mama, you know you need to stop."

"Me? Girl, you need to quit playing with yourself. You ain't give that a man a key for nothing and he ain't spending nights over here all the time and shit just cause y'all *friends.*"

Samantha whipped around with a combative look in her eyes, "Mind ya business, Mama."

Her mother returned the ferocious glare, "You keep bullshitting, Mama going show you how you get a man."

Placing her hand on her hip with an agitated tone, "No thank you this coming from a single woman, I think not."

"I told you I can get him. You a grown woman, it's on your ass to keep him."

* * *

6 a.m. on the head. At the corner of 34th and Wabash an early edition Ford sat empty on the desolate block. Scripture stood in the shadows clutching his .45 watching the car as the sun began to peak through the clouds. It had only been ten minutes since he had made the call to the Correlli family when and where they could find the old man they'd kidnapped. Scripture stood in secrecy as he watched a blue Cadillac pull up behind the car and park. Charlie sat behind the wheel as Freddy Fingers climbed out and approached the car. His eyes scanned the block as he opened the car's door, reached in, and grabbed the keys from the ignition. Walking toward the back of the car and opening the trunk, Freddy Fingers stared down into the trunk. The old man lay tied up with a cloth bag tied around his head. Freddy Fingers brushed his fingers through his goatee as he looked back at Charlie. He turned back toward the trunk, reached into his pocket jacket, and removed a switchblade. He reached in and cut the hood from the old man's face and threw it on the ground. Staring down at the old man's face beaten in and bleeding from the mouth, the old man looked up with a newfound bliss in his eyes when he realized that he was being saved, he wasn't going to die in the trunk. Freddy Fingers smiled at the old man.

"Everything going to be alright, I'm here now," Freddy pronounced with an affectionate tone. The old man sighed, Freddy Fingers plummeted his chest with the switchblade. The old man yelled out into the night as his blood splattered on Freddy Fingers face and neck. The final jab into his jugular broke the blade into his neck. He dropped the handle of the broken switchblade on top of the old man's slashed frame and slammed the trunk closed. Scripture lit a cigarette watching as Freddy Finger's climbed into the car and sped off.

***

Lying back relaxed with nothing but a towel covering her solid frame the steam penetrated her skin as so many contradicting thoughts flooded her mind. After the dinner, Monique had with Lil Larry at her place the other day she didn't know what to think or how to feel. She was having guilty thoughts, and not because they had done anything, but the fact that she enjoyed herself more than she thought she would have. The dinner turned into breakfast. They talked and laughed the whole night through. Then, he cooked breakfast for them. They ate and ended it with a warm hug then he left. Feelings were stirring up that conflicted with her love for Short Stack. She inhaled, exhaled, and then stood to leave. She exited the steam room to dress. Upon entering the changing room she found her clothing cut into shreds and her shoes missing. "What the fuck?"

She said under her breath not really believing what she was seeing. Picking up the shreds of cloth and examing closer to see if it really was her clothes, clutching tighter at her towel she snatched the door open and barged from the dressing area. Upon reaching an employee she approached with one of her arms swinging wildly.

"Get me a fucking manager!"

"Excuse me?" A confused and frightened young girl exclaimed staring back wide-eyed.

"Don't give me that excuse me shit, bitch go get a manager...Now!" Monique watched as the young lady rushed off. She felt bad for disrespecting the lady; after all, it wasn't her fault. The manager quickly returned.

"Is there a problem ma'am?" The manager a short middle-aged Puerto Rican woman asked looking just as confused as the young lady had.

"Is there a problem? Are you serious? Do you not see me standing here in nothing but a towel?"

"Yes ma'am I see that where are your clothes?"

"My clothes?" Monique's bright yellow face turned a flush red, her nose flared as she threw the shredded clothes at the manager hitting her in the face.

"Now hold on there, Ms." The manager says as she approached Monique in an aggressive manner. Monique stepped back holding her towel underneath her arms she balled up her fists and stood in a boxer's stance. The manager wasn't afraid she stood eye to eye with Monique anger peering from her eyes she spoke in a hostile tone.

"Now I don't know what happened to your clothes and I will do whatever I can to help you resolve this problem, but it won't be any more of the foul language or throwing shit in my face."

Although still upset Monique relaxed and apologised to the woman.

"I truly am sorry Miss. It's just that I don't know what's going on, this makes no sense why would someone do something like this to me?"

"I don't know but come with me sweetie; we'll get you something to wear out of here." The manager says as she takes Monique by the arm and hugs her in a comforting manner escorting her toward the back office. The manager sent an employee to a nearby department store to buy Monique something to wear. While the employee was gone she made a phone call to Sandra, Phil-Good's wife, and explained the entire ordeal. Monique was furious, and Sandra offered to meet her down at the bathhouse Sandra told her that it was okay and she would be fine. Fifth-teen minutes later they hung up and the employee returned with a simple summer dress, matching bra, panties, and a pair of matching sandals. She quickly changed thanked both the women for the clothes and their kindness and exited the bathhouse. As she walked down the street toward her car, she held her mouth in shock. Looking at her car, she found the seats, the steering wheel, both doors, and all four wheels had all been removed.

* * *

A table covered with several handguns, a shotgun, a box of shells, clips, a box of dynamite, and two cocktail bombs. The Madiassa boy sat at the table loading clips entrenched in sweat. Freddy Fingers stepped from the bathroom with a smirk across his face. This was right up his alley it was the fact that he liked the thought of violence so much it was just the rush of something exciting possibly about to go down and he was a part of the direct cause of it.

"Ready for a rampage, kid?" Freddy asked as he chuckled, picking up a grenade and tossing it in the hair, and catching it as if it were a baseball.

"How is this gonna look to the Corelli's? You butchered the old man." Charlie tried his best to keep his cool but it was hard. Freddy Fingers didn't tell him he was going pull this the Trenton crew was fine to pick off one by one, but going against the Corelli's was more than he was willing to sign up for.

"Calm down, kid. Stick to the story and the Corelli's will take care of those spooks for you."

"Yeah, I hear you. The same shit you said this morning. They gotta be smarter than that. I don't see them buying it."

"Trust me, kid, they're not gonna take those jigs word over ours. Now instead of you going on a personal vendetta, you got two families going to bat for you."

"Or I got not only the Trenton crew coming at me over Danny, 'cause as long as you believe that hell is hot, they coming for blood. I got the fucking Corelli's coming about the old man, and there ain't no way in hell Ira's buying that we found the old man dead in the trunk."

Freddy rolled the grenade across the table and snatched Charlie by his collar snatching him to his feet, "Don't you fucking back out on me now, kid. You asked for my help and I gave it to you. Stick to the story and we'll have 'em all eating out of our hands. You got it?"

Charlie yanked away from Freddy's grasp, slid the last bullet into the clip, popped the clip into the gun, cocked it back, and stuffed it in his pants. All he knew was that if things went downhill, he would kill Freddy Fingers first.

"Yeah, I got it."

***

Monique lay face down on the couch with a pillow covering her head, ignoring the phone as it rang for what seemed like the hundredth time. She had stopped answering it, frustrated because every time she picked it up it was the same female voice cursing her—telling her that she was dumb for being faithful to Short Stack. The torture would only get worse, then the caller would hang up before Monique could reply. Although Monique wasn't afraid or intimidated, she was inclined to believe that it would only get worse. After she filed a police report about her car, she called Short Stack in Indiana and told him what happened. She did have to call Sandra back to come pick her up and give her a ride home. When she walked into her home she found nothing there, but a single couch and one phone. Everything else had been taken. Holes had been punched in all the walls. The words 'whore' and 'bitch' had been carved into the walls and floors. All the food from the kitchen had been stripped from the cupboards and thrown about the kitchen. When she looked into the other bedrooms all of the mattresses and sheets had been ripped and shredded. The upstairs bedroom windows were all shattered, and broken glass covered every inch of the floor. She slid the door to her walk-in closet open to find her closet bare. All of her designer dresses and shoes were gone and Short Stack's clothes had all been torn to shreds. Fear actually did pierce her spine; she felt her stomach turn flips as she fought back the vomit. It was sickening to think that someone had violated her privacy, her home, the place where she and her man slept. She immediately called Phil-Fine and told him what happened.

After hearing what happened he sent Lil-Larry over to take her to a hotel and stay with her until Short Stack got back in town. Being stubborn, she tried to send Lil-Larry away and told him that she wouldn't run out of her own home. After a long argument, he finally left, but before leaving he made her hold on to his gun and promised to be back after the meeting if Short Stack wasn't home by then. It had been three hours since Lil-Larry had left and the phone calls still hadn't stopped. She was wishing that she hadn't been so eager to send him off, as she realized that it she let her pride get the best of her she really didn't want to be alone. She had had enough. She needed fresh air. Phil-Fine had someone drop off a car so she could get around. She was grateful for that. Monique loved

Short Stack and trusted him, but he would have a lot of explaining to do when he got home. *All this foolishness had to be another woman on the side.* She stepped outside to leave and when she opened the car door, the front seat was covered in blood. A dead cat lay across the front seat. She screamed at the top of her lungs and ran to a neighbor's house. Monica Harris, Samantha's mother sat in a parked car two blocks away laughing.

* * *

On the other side of town in a basement of a two-flat apartment building that Danny owned, Danny sat in silence as he listened to Scripture tell what went down with the drop-off. They had just gotten word that the Palm Inn had been bombed. It was a financial loss, but what could he do? He was just glad they did it when the building was empty. All the lieutenants from the Trenton crew were present and a few soldiers Danny didn't recognize. Phil-Fine stood with his back against the wall taking it all in. Danny hated the situation, but he respected it. Being confined to the wheelchair, he knew it was still Phil-Fine's show and he was just there for moral support. Randy shot pool with Uncle Jermaine. Randy would serve as Phil-Fine's General and help guide his next moves. Uncle Jermaine was there to help with what advice he could, but he was scheduled to catch his plane back out to L.A. later tonight. The IRS was still on his ass. He still hadn't gotten that warrant cleared.

Rodney Pipe and Uncle Short Stack came home early when they got the wire about what went down. They would both be his lieutenants since they both had been through the policy war with white gangsters back in 1905. Bird didn't know him, but he came highly recommended— heard he had done his bid with Pops. He was Phil-Fine's third lieutenant. Another unfamiliar face was Chuck, who also had done his bid with Pops. All Danny knew about him was that he had ridden with Scripture when he snatched the old man. Lil-Larry and Boy-Boy were also there. So Lil-Larry, Boy-Boy, and Chuck would all be soldiers. The army was assembled. Now, could they come up with a plan that would keep them all alive and not lose the business at the same time?

* * *

Giovanni's was packed. Ira and two of his lieutenants crowded a table with Paul Corelli, the older of the Corelli brothers, and three of his lieutenants. They sat drinking red wine and slurping fresh oysters and mussels. Soldiers and hired guns from both families filled the rest of the room drinking and talking amongst themselves, waiting for orders from their superiors. Paul stood and spoke to Ira in his ear in a whispered tone.

"If he ain't did nothing wrong, where's the kid?"

"It's like I told you, he feels responsible, so he's out in the streets trying to make it right."

Paul impatiently tapped the table with his fingers, "That little stunt with blowing up the niggers penny gambling spot doesn't prove he ain't provoke the old man's death."

Ira placed his hand over his chest offended, "What are you saying? That you take the word of those bastards over a pizon?"

"All I'm saying is, why would they bring the deal to us? Mind you, after they had been provoked in the first place by that nephew of yours and still not shed any blood, then turn around and do him in? It just doesn't make sense. Just cough up the kid, let me look him in the eye and see for myself where his heart is at?"

"Look, Paul, we go back a long way ..."

Ira stopped short as he glanced toward the kitchen and saw Freddy Fingers standing in the doorway.

Jumping from the table and trekking towards the kitchen Irta spat out, "Hold on, Paul. Let me go get some answers. I'll be right back."

"This fucking guy ..." Paul exclaimed angrily as he stabbed his fork into the piece of undercooked steak cracking the plate down the middle.

Ira ignored the comment never breaking stride en route to the kitchen. Freddy Fingers stood over a stove with veal frying in a skillet. He took a knife and fork, cut a piece, then blew steam from the meat and stuffed it into his mouth. Talking as he chewed, he muttered, "Shit's getting out of hand, Ira."

"You don't fucking say! What the hell happened? You were supposed to be the kid's conscience."

Freddy Fingers continued eating from the skillet. He had made up his mind that it was every man for themselves. The Corelli's weren't buying the story and it was no way he was going down for it. He pulled a cork from a bottle of wine and began drinking from the bottle as he clutched freshly baked bread with his other hand. "Look, Ira, he's your fucking nephew, so I backed his play. He wanted to put the blame all on the Coloreds, so after he chopped the old man up, it was nothing I could do. It was back his play or take him out. Shit, what would you have had me do?"

Slamming both palms down on the table, Ira's face turned cherry red, "Fuck! I fucking knew it! You did the right thing. We keep with the story and do our damnedest to get to the kid before the Corelli's or the Trenton's. We put everything we got into wiping the Trenton crew out, I mean nobody fucking lives. Wipe your mouth and get out there. Show your condolences to Paul for the old man."

* * *

Charlie stood on the corner of 39th watching a Trenton policy bank as two pick-up men exited with the afternoon's deposit. He watched the men climb into the car and pull off. "Fuck the money!" He thought one more piece to the puzzle was taken care of he advanced on Rodney Pipe. Quick calculated strides across the street toward Rodney Pipe with a gun in hand he raised and opened fire just as Rodney Pipe turned towards him. Fire leapt from the pistol as Rodney Pipe felt the inferno grow in his stomach elevating his firearm and squeezing the shots rung out like thunder. Stumbling as he stepped back, crouched he felt his shirt get damp and cling to his frame. Charlie took cover hunkered by a parked car and continued firing. Rodney Pipe held his balance as his back pressed against the wall clutching his stomach as blood ran through his fingers.

"How did I let this pussy get the drop on me?" Rodney spat out to himself...his thoughts raced, *"How the fuck I'm going get out of this?, running low on ammo, them punks with me done ran, and it won't be long before the law...."* He felt faint, the roar from sirens blared through the air in the distance. Peeking around the corner from his hiding place quickly looking in the direction from where the

firing was coming from he caught a glimpse of Charlie making a dash towards his car. Rodney Pipe gripped his stomach as his blood ran through his fingers and his vision blurred. Staggering towards Charlie, letting loose shots. Charlie crouched as the bullets whizzed over his head. He reached his car, snatched the door open and threw it into drive, hit the gas, and pulled off with the door still open, swerving as he drove with his head low, bullets shattered his rear window he turned the corner almost on two wheels. Rodney Pipe stuffed the gun into his pants and buttoned up his jacket. He turned and walked to his car. Once he heard police sirens behind him quickly approaching, he headed toward the El station bypassing his vehicle he needed to blend in with the crowd.

*   *   *

A chubby, six-foot tall plain-clothes policeman by the name of Detective "Rusty" Bill sat in his unmarked police car in front of the burned-down Palm Inn. He had been getting word through his snitches that something big was brewing between the Coloreds and Italians. He needed to stop it before it happened. No matter what he did he was always a step behind, he should've been able to prevent this. Although it was in a Colored neighborhood, he didn't like things happening in his prescient that he didn't give the okay for. He started his engine, ready to make his rounds through the South Side to check out all the Policy King's known hangouts. When an all-cars bulletin came out over the police radio, he spun a U-turn in the other direction and headed toward the disturbance.

*   *   *

Corelli's soldiers had witnessed the whole thing. They were staked out at the end of the block waiting to move on any of the Trenton gang. Two cars deep, they spotted Charlie but thought they would wait and let him eliminate the one from the Trenton crew. Then they would split up, have one car follow the money and one car follow Charlie. But when Charlie botched the hit, they were forced to let the money car go and each take a man to follow.

The car following Rodney Pipe pulled several blocks ahead. The passenger hopped out and walked back in Rodney Pipe's direction. Trying not to look suppositious, he walked with his head down. The car circled the block and was once again behind Rodney Pipe. Knowing he wasn't out of the woods yet because the sounds of the police sirens were still approaching, Rodney Pipe unbuttoned his suit jacket as his trigger finger caressed the butt of his gun. Corelli's crony, who was quickly approaching, was too eager to draw. Rodney Pipe spotted him through the crowd as he reached for his pistol. The two were at least a block and a half apart. Rodney Pipe was a crack shot. He yanked his gun from his pants, took quick aim, and squeezed. A woman screamed as the bullet smacked the man's chest plate and his frame fell back on top of her as she held her baby. Rodney Pipe rushed to the woman and rolled the body from on top of her. She continued to scream as she scooted away, clutching her baby and watching as Rodney Pipe squeeze two more shots into his face, the man's face cracked down the middle as the crowd scrambled and dispersed. Rodney snatched the clip from the gun, dropped it to the ground, and popped another one in. A car driving at a high speed headed right toward him. With no time to run or jump out of the way of the approaching vehicle he began firing at the car, multiple shots into the windshield the car swerved and hit a wall. Now losing more and more blood by the minute, Rodney staggered toward the car as the chubby white man hopped from the car and took cover. Rodney raised his gun to fire when from behind he heard gunshots and bullets whizzing in his direction. The pain in his stomach was so severe he hadn't felt the bullet hit him in the back underneath his shoulder. He spun and began firing at the car quickly approaching and the driver hanging from the window still fired at him.

The chubby man who'd jumped from the crashed vehicle ducked from his hiding place and yelled out, "Police, drop your weapon."

Rodney ignored the order and kept firing at the oncoming car. Police squad cars finally reached the scene surrounding Rodney Pipe. The Detective took aim and fired, squeezing off six shots into Rodney Pipe's back until he hit the cement face first and died. Outnumbered, Corelli's soldier threw his weapon from the car and surrendered.

* * *

Here he was bullshitting again. His old lady was going through some non-sense he couldn't understand. Where was he? Sitting in Samantha's house yet again trying to escape the drama of his life at least for a few hours anyway. He had missed her and this might be his only time to see her again for a long time. With the war going on with the Italians, it would be too dangerous to keep coming by. He stood in her bedroom with his back against the wall watching her model the new dresses he had bought her while he was out of town. She spun in a circle, smiling as she admired the new dress. She rushed toward him and fell into his arms hugging him.

"Oh thank you, Short Stack. It's just beautiful."

Their eyes met as he felt her breasts press against his chest. She leaned in and pressed her lips against his lips. Her tongue slid into his mouth as he placed his hand on the small of her back. She nibbled at his lip as she pulled back. They once again stared into one another's eyes. He ran his hand down the side of her face.

"You're welcome." He gently pushed her away. She stepped back with her hands on her hips. He walked out of her room and out of her house. She stood in silence as she realized that she had overstepped her bounds. She hadn't meant to it just happened, it felt right. First, she felt anger that he had left without saying a word she kicked the walls and pounded with her fists like a child throwing a temper tantrum...that emotion was quickly replaced with regret and sadness she slumped against the wall in a corner of her room as she realized that she may never see him again, a single tear dropped from her eye and rolled down her face.

* * *

Charlie needed to get off the streets and more importantly out of Chicago. There was no one he could really reach out to. He'd burnt all his bridges, his uncle probably would have him killed just to keep the peace with the Corelli family. No doubt word was out that he fucked up the hit on one of the Trenton boys. The only choice he had was to reach out to the very person he knew might be his very demise. He pulled to the curb, hopped out, and stepped into the phone booth. He snatched the phone from the receiver.

"Hello, operator, I'd like to make a collect call."

* * *

Paul hung up the phone and then whispered to his top lieutenant. After hearing his boss's instructions, he rushed off. Paul pulled his gun from his holster, opened the chamber, spun it, closed it, and placed it back into the holster things were finally looking his way. That phone call would change the entire demographic of the blood bath that was going on in the streets if handled properly, it would change to his benefit. He rushed to his car followed by his bodyguards. He stepped outside and climbed into his car. The vehicle bolted from the curb.

* * *

Short Stack rode down Cottage Grove. He wasn't even home a good week and had some bullshit to deal with. He was almost in tears thinking about what he had to do. He pulled the car up to the curb as Heaven and Roberta got into his car. They were some old friends who owed him a favor; now it was time to pay. So he had Lil-Larry reach out to them. They rode for about fifteen minutes until they came up to Samantha's neighborhood. Before he even turned the corner to her block, he spotted her and her mother coming out of the corner store.

Short Stack spoke in a heart-shattering whisper, "*That's them!*"

Before he could even pull the car over and park, Heaven and Roberta jumped out and attacked Samantha and her mother. Letting the blows rain down on their heads and face, the two women didn't see it coming. Samantha and her mother tried to fight back, but they were no match for Heaven and Roberta. Blow after blow from a sock filled with quarters, the women's blood covered the streets as chunks of flesh hung from their faces!

Short Stack climbed from the car and stood over the women. He knelt down, grabbing a handful of Samantha's hair. He yanked her head back so they were eye to eye. Short Stack felt his heart shatter looking into Samantha's eyes he read hurt and confusion when she realized he was the cause of the attack. She knew she overstepped her bounds by kissing him but never imagined he would take it to this degree. She started crying uncontrollably as she plead, "Short Stack, why?"

"Stay the fuck away from my woman, you coward ass bitches!"

Short Stack and the two women climbed back into his car and drove off, leaving Samantha and her mother squirming on the ground tainted with their own blood. After Monique had confronted Short Stack about the telephone calls and the blood in her car, he had a friend of his at the phone company check the telephone records. He learned that Samantha's mother had been calling and threatening Monique. *That old bitch had to be doing that shit 'cause Samantha told her to.* At least that's what he thought. Monica had never told her daughter about the threats and what she had done to Monique's home and car. She thought she was doing what needed to be done to make her daughter happy.

* * *

Freddy Fingers rushed toward the South Side of Chicago heading in Charlie's direction. He had gotten word from a lieutenant from the Corelli crew where he could find Charlie. He hardly believed his ears that Charlie would make a move as risky as this. Desperate times called for desperate actions he was just glad that he was able to flip someone from the Corelli family to give up the information. They had planned to call the Madiassa family but they wanted to be the ones to get him off the streets first to question Charlie about the botched drop-off for the old man. They didn't have to call the Madiassa's at all but as a courtesy to prevent any further bad blood between the two families. But Freddy had intentions of his own. He had to get there before Paul before the kid spilled the beans about him being the cause of the old man's death and him fanning the flames of the war that was going on.

* * *

She had to admit he did make shit happen and took good care of her when he needed to. She wasn't going to let him off the hook that easy though. She wanted to believe that this Samantha chick was just a friend but if she was just a friend why hadn't he told her about her or introduced the two of them. She'd decided if she wasn't going to leave him it didn't make sense to keep thinking about it. Short Stack hadn't been home for twenty-four hours yet and had the place looking better than new. Monique reclined on her couch reading and enjoying her new living room furniture. She missed her old stuff, but she loved the new layout even better. It would take a few days for the fresh paint smell to leave, but she could deal with it. The floors and windows had all been replaced. She had to admit the place looked better than it did before. Short Stack spared no expense. Tomorrow he would take her to get a new wardrobe and car shopping. A knock at the door took her from her thoughts. She went to answer it.

"Who is it?"

"It's me!"

Short Stack said from the other side of the door. She started not to open the door thinking he was being silly knocking when all he had to do was use his key. She yanked the door open to find her front porch and yard filled with red, yellow, and white roses. Short Stack was bent down on one knee holding a ring.

"Monique!"

"Yes, Obadiah."

Short Stack, with tears in his eyes, paused before speaking with sentiment in his voice, "Will you marry me?"

With a lump in her throat and tears in her eyes, she wiped the tears from his, and answered, "Yes, Obadiah. Yes baby, I will marry you!"

Short Stack stood up and then took Monique into his arms and kissed her with more ecstasy than he ever had. Wrapping her arms around his neck as he grasped her ass she kissed him back with just as much emotion as he had.

* * *

Charlie was far from dumb. Although he had reached out to Paul, he knew he was still pissed and there was no telling how this might play out. To say he wasn't scared would be a lie to himself if he did nothing else like to at least be honest with himself. He told Paul to meet him across town at a Tavern in two hours. It was getting late; the sun had gone down. He had to get on the ball if he expected to make it there before Paul did. He pulled into an alley and rolled down the window.

"Hey, you want to make fifty bucks?" he yelled out to the bum lying on the ground.

The man got up and staggered over to the car.

* * *

Freddy Fingers was in a cold sweat as he talked to himself aloud. He headed to the meet-up spot where Charlie was waiting. This was better than he thought; the Corelli's hadn't made it yet. He spotted Charlie's car sitting on the corner, and the driver looking around nervously. Freddy Fingers parked half a block away. No sooner than he reached the passenger door of Charlie's car, he put the barrel of the gun to the back of the man's head and pulled the trigger. The right side of his head exploded leaving blood, brains, and particles of skull splattered against the inside of the windshield. From his jacket pocket, he pulled out a Molotov bomb, lit it, and threw it on the front seat next to the body. He walked back to his car, hopped in, and drove off. Three blocks away he watched the car explode into flames through his rear-view window.

* * *

Jermaine exited the meat market he stopped by to pick up some fresh hot hog head cheese he was craving as he walked toward his car. He was on his way to get Tania. Their flight would be leaving in a little under an hour. A pair of arms suddenly gripped hold of Jermaine's arms. From pure reflex, he elbowed his attacker in the face busting his lip, but his grip remained tight, Jermaine jerked from left to right, managing to slip out of his coat. Running down the street, his assailant fired his weapon. Three shots rang out missing Jermaine as he ducked down behind a car. A woman screeched out in fear panic ensued as people scattered to get away from the firing. Jermaine took a deep breath, pulled his gun, and charged toward the man firing. Two shots pierced the attacker in the chest. The man fell as Jermaine stood over him letting loose until his clip was empty. Lifting his shirt, he placed his gun in the front of his pants. Glancing down the block, he saw people ducking and running from the shooting. Walking back towards his car, his heart pounded from the rush of excitement mixed with fear. Jermaine hated using his gun; he didn't fear it just didn't like it. But it was sometimes a necessity. He had forgotten all about his hog head cheese that he dropped during the scuffle. Stopping in front of the meat market he became more upset that his hog head cheese had been stepped on by someone running from the commotion. Checking once more down the block towards where the gun shoot-out had taken place to make sure no one else was lurking behind any buildings itching to gun him down he bent down and picked up his bag of food looking at it he dropped the bag and climbed into his car, he slowly drove away from the scene.

* * *

THE RETURN OF THE GANGSTER

The year was 1930. The policy wars were still going strong. It was no longer about Corelli's grandfather or Charlie's vendetta. The Italians wanted the numbers rackets and were willing to spill blood to get it. Danny was now out of his wheelchair. Although walking with a cane for a short while, he was back on his feet. There was no repairing the Palm Inn, so Danny purchased a new building a few doors down. He had it remodeled and named it The Diamond Deluxe. It was filled with people and the band was playing. As Phil-Good and Danny entered The Diamond Deluxe, the room exploded in applause and cheers.

Phil-Good couldn't enjoy his coming home celebration. He was happy to be out but it was too much to deal with it was no time to party people were coming at his family and his livelihood so instead of feeling joyous he felt a deep annoyance talking through clenched teeth.

"Thank you, everybody, but it's not necessary."

"Now you knew we were gonna do this pops."

"Yeah I know, but *I told you not to*, I told *your brother not to*, I told *Jermaine and Carlin* not to. *What?* I've been gone that long that *don't nobody listen to me no more?*"

"No, it's not that, Pops."

Phil-Good grabbed Danny by the collar in annoyance and shoved him, "Get everybody in the back so I can get filled in on what's what around here."

* * *

Lil-Larry was bitter. Yeah, working with Short Stack he had made much more money than he ever had working with Blue Ball, but damn the money. He wanted Monique she was all he could think of. It took everything in him not to at least drive by the restaurant where she worked to try and catch a glimpse of her. He knew he felt something that night they spent together he was pretty damn sure she had too. Things changed once Short Stack came home Monique told him that she was engaged to marry Short Stack and she didn't think it would be fair to keep seeing him. She even went so far as to ask him to stop coming by the restaurant to eat. As far as he was concerned, he was down, but he wasn't out. He sat on the couch as Samantha curled up next to him. He'd met Short Stack at Samantha's home a few times and was slightly familiar with Samantha but never thought he'd be spending time with her in her home. Things changed, how everything was going with Monique and Short Stack he had to find a way to make it work in his favor and Samantha just might be the key to that. It was strange, but he somehow found solace in hanging out with her. She was heartbroken and confused about Short Stack, but what could she do? She tried to get messages to him, but he never called her back or stopped by to talk and she didn't dare stop by The Diamond Deluxe to see him. So when Lil-Larry said that he had a plan that would get Monique away from Short Stack forever, she was more than eager to do whatever he asked.

* * *

The war was still going strong and it didn't look as if it would be winding down any time soon. Phil-Good was home and had resumed control of the numbers racket. Freddy Fingers plopped an olive into his mouth as he sat at the bar downing dry martinis. Ira was playing bartender in one of the after-hour clubs he owned. The place was closed. The staff was cleaning to go home for the morning. Freddy Fingers gestured at a bottle behind the bar. Ira turned, grabbed the bottle of olives, and handed them to Freddy. It had been a little under a month since the explosion of Charlie's car. Ira had no clear way of knowing who had done it, both the Corelli's and the Trenton's were suspect. It could've been either. He didn't have the finances or the patience to go to war with both at the same time, so he chose to leave the personal beefs dead with his nephew and focus on the money. With a mouth full of olives Freddy Fingers said, "I swear to fucking Christ I'm just glad you taking this thing with Charlie as good as you is."

Ira placed his hand on Freddy Fingers shoulder, "What am I gonna do? I warned him. But regardless of what's going on, I got to earn."

Freddy Fingers coughed up flim and spit it on the floor behind the bar. "It's taking me by surprise that Phil-Good ain't called for a sit-down by now."

"Who knows what's on his mind, he can't actually think he can win."

* * *

With the war effort costing them so much, having to hire more soldiers, guns and ammunition, court cases, funerals, and taking care of fallen men's families. This was taking a toll on Phil-Good mentally and financially. So to keep money rolling in he sent Bird and Chuck down to East Chicago to continue what Short Stack and Rodney Pipe had started before Rodney was killed. He also let Danny and Randy continue with the Jamaican connection. Phil-Fine basically stepped back once Phil-Good took back control of the crew. Jermaine was scheduled to turn himself in sometime this week. Short Stack still did his thing as usual and Scripture was no longer Danny's personal bodyguard, he worked on special assignments for Phil-Good. Phil-Good knew he had to put this to bed, soon he just hadn't figured out how yet.

* * *

The bagman for Paul sat in his car with his pistol on his lap clutching a brown paper bag. Detective "Rusty" Bill pulled up coming from the opposite direction and parked parallel to the bagman's car. The bagman throws the brown paper bag into Rusty Bill's window. He catches the bag and throws it on the back seat. With a greedy smile, he said, "It's kind of heavy."

The bag man irritated by Rusty Bill snidely responded, "The boss said for that kind of money no room for fuck ups."

Before Rusty Bill could answer the bagman threw the car into drive and sped off.

* * *

From the information that he'd received from Roberta and Heaven about how Short Stack acted when they beat Samantha and her mom down, Lil Larry knew that Short Stack was still sweet on Samantha. Even if she didn't know it, that's what he would play off of. After feeding Samantha drink after drink, she was finally in a relaxed state of mind where she could do what was needed of her. He'd told her that he had talks with Short Stack and he wanted to see her but didn't know how to go about it, being what he had done to her he didn't think she would forgive him. Samantha didn't believe it. She had known Short Stack for too long and that didn't sound like him. She didn't see him taking anything back he had ever said or done. But she needed desperately to believe that he would for her. So she let Lil Larry not only feed her the alcohol to get her to confront Short Stack, but she also fed into his lies. So it was set. He was to drop her off at The Diamond Deluxe to meet Short Stack. Lil Larry had another dilemma, he had to get Short Stack there. He pulled over, and Samantha hesitated turning towards him.

"Take me back home Larry." She said with fear in her eyes. Lil Larry attempted to hide his disappointment. "What? Take you home? We done came too far now to turn back. You done built up the courage to come, plus he on his way."

"I don't know Larry it doesn't seem right, you sure he wanted to see me?"

"Trust me, baby girl, what I got to gain from lying to you? Think about it do you know how disappointed he'll be to come down here and not see you?" Samantha wanted deeply to believe that Short Stack asked to see her and he wanted to see her as much as she wanted to see him. She partially smiled at Lil Larry, opened the door, stepped out of the car, and walked into the building. This goofy broad going to spoil everything he thought as he pulled off to execute the next segment of his scheme.

* * *

Later that night, Phil-Good, Danny, and Randy all sat at a table at Phil-Good's house drinking liquor and playing cards.

Phil-Good took a swallow of his scotch, "I got some fucked up news about half an hour ago. I mean if it ain't one thang it's a muthafucking nother!"

Danny shuffled the cards, "What is it, Pops?"

"Bird called me collect from jail. He caught a murder charge."

"What?" Randy exclaimed, wide-eyed as he knocked over the bottle of liquor from the shock of the news.

"Watch what you doing nigga!" Danny bent over and picked up the bottle.

"Yeah, I called down to get the scoop from his partner Chuck and he said it was over an argument with a drunken old man over a five-dollar bet. Randy, take a couple of the boys and drive down. Make sure shit still moving that way."

"No doubt."

"Danny, make sure Bird got a good lawyer."

"I'm on it, Pops."

* * *

Monique sat on the couch with her feet propped up on the coffee table. Short Stack lay on the couch with his head on her lap. She rubbed his scalp as they discussed the wedding and possible honeymoon spots. The phone rang. Monique got up and walked across the room then snatched the receiver from the base.

"Hello."

"Hello, Short Stack there?" A familiar male voice asked.

Monique felt anger build up in her stomach but tried not to reveal it on her face. She instantly recognized the voice as Lil Larry. She wanted to lie and say no, he wasn't home, but thought twice about it. They *were* in the middle of a war. Although he kept her sheltered from that as much as possible, she wasn't naive.

"Telephone, Obadiah," Monique yelled.

He walked over to her, took the phone, and poked out his lips playfully for a kiss. She smiled and then pecked her lips against his. Before she pulled back, he playfully bit her bottom lip.

"Ouch, boy why are you biting and stuff?" she asked with a smile, walking back to the couch.

"What I tell you 'bout calling me Obadiah?"

"Okay, I got you."

He spoke into the phone. "Hello."

Monique sat thumbing through a magazine trying not to appear as if she was listening.

Lil Larry spoke methodically, "I was over at Diamond Deluxe 'bout a half hour ago, and ya' girl was up there acting a fool."

Short Stack knew immediately who he was talking about, but couldn't say her name aloud. He knew Monique was listening.

"What do you want me to do? I don't care."

"I don't know, just thought you should know. She's asking for you and shit. Cursing folks out, said she ain't leaving till she talks to you. I would've handled it myself, but I had something to see to first. Plus, I know you ain't want nobody from there to handle her. Ain't no telling what might happen if somebody put hands on her. You know it's gonna turn out real ugly."

The last thing he needed was to be in the midst of this shit. He was finally getting things back right with Monique.

"How long before you can get back over there?"

"I'm damn near to the hundreds, it's gonna be a while."

The hundreds were the hundred blocks of Chicago, which were at least twenty-five to thirty minutes away from The Diamond Deluxe. Short Stack was ten minutes away.

"Fuck it, I'm on it. Thanks for the call, man."

The phone went dead. Short Stack hung up, looked over at Monique, and smiled. She stood, rolled her eyes angrily, and stormed upstairs slamming the bedroom door closed. He laughed and then marched upstairs. He grabbed the bedroom door handle and twisted it. The door was locked.

"Open this door, girl. Stop being silly."

"Just go, Obadiah."

"It ain't gonna take long."

"You're a liar, I don't believe you."

"Babe, I promise."

She snatched the door open. "I don't think you should go, something doesn't feel right. I'm begging you, Obadiah stay here with me."

He laughed, grabbed both sides of her face softly, and kissed her lips.

"Right back. Give me an hour, okay?"

"An hour?"

"Maybe less." He turned and ran down the stairs.

She yelled out, "I love you!"

"Love you too, babe, see you in a few."

She heard the door slam closed. She rushed across the bedroom and looked out the window as she watched him climb into his car and speed off.

* * *

After hanging up the phone, Lil Larry stepped away from the phone booth then climbed into his car, and drove around the block to The Diamond Deluxe. He parked and rushed inside. It wouldn't be long before Short Stack would be there. He needed to hurry and get Samantha out before he arrived. His initial plan was to gun them both down. But after spending time with her, it was easy to see why Short Stack was so soft for her. She had a good soul. Upon entering and walking across the room he spotted her sitting in a corner booth with Boy-Boy. "Shit!" he thought to himself. *Another fucking witness to worry about.* He didn't know how much she had told him or if she had told him at all. He nodded at Boy-Boy to meet him across the room. Boy-Boy slid from the booth and strolled over to where Lil Larry was waiting.

"What's up?" Boy-Boy asked with a menacing smile smeared across his face.

"Shit, what you doing up in here with her?"

Boy-Boy paused before answering; "Now you know damn well we ain't come here together. She was here when I walked in."

"Well, what am I supposed to think? I walk in and y'all hugged up together laughing and shit."

"Get on with yo' exaggerating ass."

"Just get her out of here, take her home. Short Stack gonna be pissed if he comes in and she here."

Boy-Boy was impervious to the remark, he scrunched his shoulders, "So, that's they're shit."

Unable to hide his anxiousness anymore Lil Larry nudged Boy-Boy's shoulder, "Just do it man, we got enough on our plates to have to deal with this bullshit. That's when something goes wrong and people get hurt."

Boy-Boy smirked, then walked back to the table and motioned for Samantha to come with him. She stood and headed toward the exit. Lil Larry turned his back as they walked past, not acknowledging her.

"Hold on, hold on, I ain't going no place!" Samantha slurred out as she stopped in her tracks and turned towards Lil Larry.

"Fuck" Lil Larry cursed under his breath. Boy-Boy grabbed her by the wrist and pulled her towards the door. She squirmed, struggled, and pulled until she had broken his grip.

"I ain't ya woman now, don't be pushing me around! I ain't leaving til' I see the mutha I came here to see. Shit nigga keeps telling me he wants to see me. Where is he at?" Samantha exclaimed as she stomped towards Lil Larry. Lil Larry kept his back turned towards her. She tapped his shoulder in the same spot over and over annoyingly.

"Larry, Larry, Larry, Larry, Larry....You don't hear me talking to you Larry?" Lil Larry smashed his glass slamming it down on the bar, furiously spun around now face to face with Samantha. Anger creased the lines on his face. Samantha stared back with just as much anger on her face. Staring up at Lil Larry, eyes bucked and rolling her neck as she spoke, "I know you ain't bring me down here on no bullshi..." Before she could get the rest of the word out Boy-Boy snatched her from her feet and carried her from the bar yelling and screaming. Lil Larry knew that the two of them spending more time together gave her more opportunities to talk and give up information if she hadn't already, but it was a chance he had to take. He was just glad she was gone. Short Stack would be there soon. Lil-Larry waited two minutes then exited. He drove around the block, got out of his car, and then walked around to his trunk. Opening the trunk, he exchanged his suit jacket for his trench coat. Removing a sawed-off shotgun from the trunk and placing it inside his coat, he closed the trunk and headed back to The Diamond Deluxe on foot.

* * *

The sun was beginning to set as Short Stack pulled up to the front of The Diamond Deluxe. He turned the car off and laid his head on the steering wheel. He was having second thoughts about getting involved. Why did he really come down, he cared about her true but he loved Monique. He needed to see her and ask her how she could do those things knowing that they would hurt him. He got out and slammed the door closed and headed toward the front entrance. Short Stack saw Lil Larry approaching so he bypassed the entrance and headed towards Lil Larry. Short Stack was pissed. How the hell was he here so quick and he claimed to be so far away? Short Stack was ready to curse him out, but once he was within arms reach of Lil Larry, Lil Larry opened his trench coat brandishing the sawed-off shotgun. He squeezed the trigger twice, filling Short Stack's frame with buckshot. Short Stack flew into the air crashing to the pavement. He was dead before he hit the ground. His nerves still shook as his legs jerked uncontrollably. Lil Larry turned and walked around the block, praying no one saw him.

* * *

Danny and Apricot stood in front of the small pond in the backyard of their home watching as the leaves fell from the trees signalling the changing of the seasons. Both stood in silence lost in their own thoughts. Without looking at Danny, Apricot spoke, "So wha yuh really think....this sittin' ah go done soon or wha?

"Real soon, babe, real soon."

"Don't be lying to me. We come to far for it." "

"Real soon, promise. Daddy got something going one way or the other real soon."

"Danny I ..."

"I'm sorry, Apricot, for the way I've been treating you these past few months."

"Don't be worrying about it."

"No, I mean I truly am sorry. I love ..."

Phil-Good burst into the yard interrupting their conversation. "Sorry, Apricot. Danny, we got to go. Something happened,"

"What's going on, Pops?" Danny asked looking startled.

"Not here, let's go."

He turned and exited the way he had come from. Danny turned to Apricot. "You understand where I'm coming from?"

"I do."

They hugged. He ran to catch up with his father. "What is it, Pops?"

Phil-Good climbed into the driver seat and Danny hopped in the passenger seat. Phil-Good pulls off.

"Danny man ..."

"What is it, Pops?" Danny was becoming more and more anxious waiting on what he knew had to be bad news.

"They just found Short Stack in front of The Diamond Deluxe shot to shit."

"Come on, Pops. It can't be."

"No witnesses, or at least none that's talking."

"So who do you think?"

"Could be either family, don't know, but that ain't all."

"What else is it?"

"Just got a call from a Detective "Rusty" Bill."

Danny shrugged his shoulders in an uncaring fashion. "Never heard of him."

"Yeah, me either, I got Carlin checking him out for me."

With his eyebrows cast down Danny placed a cigarette between his lips, "What does he want?"

"Said Ira got him to act as a mediator between us."

"You trust him?"

Never moving his eyes from the road his words were doused in venom, "What the fuck kind of question is that?"

"What? You don't think we should go?"

"Yeah, we going, but it's gonna have to wait, till after we deal with this shit."

* * *

The Mayflower Baptist Church on 49th and South Parkway was empty except for Blue Ball who was standing at the pulpit when Phil-Good entered.

"How did you know I was here?" Blue Ball asked.

"A lucky guess. It was either here or riding around with a shotgun."

"How you know I wasn't riding around?"

"I didn't. That's why I got people riding around looking for your car. If it's any consolation I'm glad you here and not riding around."

"You know the funny thing, man?"

"What?"

"You would think I would hate the bastard that did it to him, but I don't."

"That ain't an easy thing to do."

"You would think so, huh? But if God doesn't will hate in your heart, it won't be there."

"Yeah, I suppose."

Blue Ball chuckled. He sat and pat the bench inviting Phil-Good to sit next to him, "You and me in the same club now, huh?" Blue Ball refers to Phil-Good's brother who had been gunned down twenty years before.

"Shit, it ain't a man alive that want membership to that club. You're welcome to stay at the house, you know if you don't want to be alone. And I'm covering all the costs of the funeral and burial."

"I appreciate that man, but there is one thing I ask."

Tilting his head forward, "Whatever, just name it?"

"The guy who killed my brother."

"Yeah."

"Can you make sure nothing happens to him?"

Leaning his head back and closing his eyes he shook his head in disbelief, "I know we in church and everything, but you got to be kidding?"

A blissful smile smothered his face, "Vengeance is mine says the Lord!"

Phil-Good was almost pleading with Blue Ball. "Blue, man, I can't ..."

Blue Ball cut him off. "Let he who is without sin cast the first stone."

Phil-Good jumped to his feet angrily standing over Blue Ball, "It was *Short Stack,* man. He was my brother, too!"

"You said anything and before you went away, you were a man of your word. I hope you returned the same man." Blue Ball stood to his feet placing a gentle hand on Phil-Good's shoulder.

"Damn, how you gonna do this to me, man?" Phil-Good shook his head in disbelief.

"However you want it, man. Come on and give me a hug, so I can get out of here."

* * *

A week had gone past and all was quiet on the street. Phil-Good had Ira get word to the detective to have both of the Italian families back off for a week, then he would agree to the meeting. It was the day of Short Stack's funeral. Jermaine had sneaked back into town to see his old friend put to rest. The streets were bumper to bumper with cars and people. Short Stack was well-liked. People from all over the community came to pay their respects, gangsters and working citizens alike. A limousine pulled in front of the church. Monique climbed from the back of the limousine followed by Tania and Jermaine. As they approached the stairs to the church, Detective "Rusty" Bill approached. Jermaine didn't know who he was, but he didn't have to know. He could sense when the law was present. Jermaine looked at the two women and said, "Go on inside, I'll be in shortly."

"Tania hesitated, then kissed him on the cheek. She turned Monique and took her by the arm, leading her up the stairs.

"Jermaine Lloyd?" Detective "Rusty" Bill spoke.

"And you are?"

He flashed a badge. "Detective Russell, call me Rusty Bill. You know why I'm here, right?"

"Yeah, and I'm sure you heard about me?"

Rusty Bill shrugged his shoulders, "Some."

"Well, from the amount that you heard, you know I'm a stand-up guy."

"From what I hear."

"Doing a favor for me goes a long way."

"I'm listening."

"Let me sit through the funeral, say bye to my old friend, then I'll turn myself in immediately after."

Rusty Bill had heard that a favor from the Policy King was worth its weight in gold, he had no intention of saying no but didn't want to come across as overly anxious either. He paused, narrowed his eyes but never waivered from eye contact with Jermaine, "I trust you Jermaine, go on inside with your wife. I ain't gonna sit around here and babysit, so I trust when I check in, in a few hours you would've done the right thing?"

Jermaine reached out his hand and shook hands with Rusty Bill.

"I owe you one, detective."

Jermaine ran up the stairs into the church.

* * *

The church was filled to capacity. People stood along the walls and in the aisles. Monique and the rest of the Crew sat up front. The soldiers sat directly behind them in the second row, Lil Larry included. He sat staring with a triumphant smirk across his face as he stared at Monique weeping. No one paid any particular attention to Lil Larry, concentrating more on Blue Ball giving the sermon. Everyone except Boy-Boy. He sat two rows back from Lil Larry he knew the truth, but he hadn't said anything. He would bring it out when the time was right ... Right in time to benefit him, that is. Blue Ball stood at the pulpit giving his sermon. Jermaine sat crying and wheezing, looking at Tania with swollen puffy eyes.

He whispered in her ear. "I can't take it, baby, I need some air."

Grace engraved on her face, "You want me to come with you?"

"Naw, I'm all right."

He went out to the porch of the church and lit a cigarette, unaware of the danger only a few feet away. Although they had got the message from Rusty Bill to lay off, Ira and Freddy Fingers couldn't let an opportunity like this pass them by. They knew everyone's defenses would be down at a funeral, so they sat across the street in a parked car, watching.

Freddy Fingers nudged Ira in his ribs with his elbow, "Is that one of 'em?"

Ira looked out the window in the direction of the church and saw Jermaine standing there smoking a cigarette. He grimaced at Freddy before speaking, "Yeah, that's one of 'em."

"Let's get 'em."

"Be cool, be cool, we don't want to scare 'em off. Start the engine."

Freddy started the car up. "Bust a U-turn and when he starts to go back in the church, *let him have it in the back!*"

* * *

Blue Ball stood at the pulpit preaching. He hadn't the slightest idea of what to say. It took all he had in him not to turn and walk away. Staring out at the crowd of sad Black faces he thought what would Short Stack do if it were him laying in that box and Short Stack had to say words about him? If Blue Ball ain't know nothing else about his brother he knew he always spoke the truth. So that's what Blue Ball did he began speaking the truth. "*Blessed are the poor in spirit for theirs is the kingdom of heaven.* It's funny, me saying those words. *Blessed are the poor in spirit for theirs is the kingdom of heaven!* What does that mean? I'll be honest with you, I don't know, but I'll tell you what it means to me! Everyone here knew my brother. He was a wealthy man, a worldly man! But he was a poor man!"

A woman from the crowd yelled out, "*Take your time!*"

Blue Ball, now yelling, panting, and swaying back and forward continued, "Come on now, stay with me, I say, he was a poor man because he was poor in spirit and poor in the spirit of the lord!"

A man from the audience let out a yell, "*Umm, hmm ...*"

Blue Ball lowered his voice almost to a whisper, "So by right, he's in heaven! *Blessed are those who mourn for they shall be comforted.* No one here mourns harder than I do, but I must be honest. I'm still seeking comfort, but I know my God is a good God."

A woman belted out, "*Come on now!*"

"*He has not forsaken me and I will be blessed!* I know there are a lot of hurt people in here today, I hurt, too! I know it's a lot of mad people ... people who want revenge ... people who want blood! But not me ... umm, umm ... *Blessed are the peacemakers, for they shall be called sons of God!*"

Another woman yelled out, "*Say it again!*"

He continued, "*I say, blessed are the peacemakers for they shall be called sons of God!* I loved my brother. Lord knows I did, but he gone and I'll miss him, but I ain't to give up my birthright for no one!"

A man cheered him on. "*I hear you, Blue Ball!*"

"It's some people here today who might not agree with me, but I don't care! *Those who are persecuted for righteousness' sake, for theirs is the kingdom of heaven!* So go 'ahead, talk about me. I know where my kingdom is!"

A man said, "*Bring it home, brother!*"

"*Blessed are you when they revile and persecute you and say—say all kinds of evil against you falsely, for my sake.* I don't care, talk about me, call me a coward. It does not matter! *I will rejoice and be exceedingly glad for great is my reward in heaven. For they persecuted the prophets who were before me!* You know what that means, don't you?"

A woman said, "*Mmm hmm ...*"

"Talk about me. They talked about men who were greater than me and they still persevered!"

The rat-a-tat-tat from a machine gun rang outside the church and car tires screeching invaded the sanctity of the church. Tania jumped up.

"*Oh my God. Jermaine!*" she yelled.

She ran toward the door and Phil-Good grabbed her from behind.

"*Wait here!*"

Phil-Good and Danny both pulled out guns and ran outside. They found Jermaine on the ground in a puddle of blood.

Tania staggered outside and let out a screeching scream. "Noooooo!"

* * *

Tania lay in bed with Sandra on one side and Charlene, Carlin's wife on the other. She couldn't stop crying, she shook uncontrollably. They were attempting to comfort her, they were afraid to leave her alone, thinking she may do something to hurt herself. Someone knocked at the door.

"It's me can I come in?" Phil-Good said from the other side of the door.

Tania sat up, anxiously yelling out, "Yes Phillip, please come in."

Phil-Good stepped in with the look of a heartbroken little boy, "You need anything? Something to eat? I can send one of the boys to get whatever you need."

Tania smiled affectionately, "No thank you, but I would like to talk to you alone for a second."

Charlene and Sandra both looked at one another, "We'll be here all night if you need anything." Sandra says as she and Charlene got up from the bed and left the room, closing the door behind them.

"What can I do for you, sweetheart?" Phil-Good said as he stood near the bedroom door fidgeting in place.

Tania patted the bed, motioning Phil-Good to come and sit down. He sat next to her as she wiped tears from her eyes. Gently, she laid her head on his shoulder.

"What is it?" Phil-Good asked. He had never felt so uncomfortable in his life. No matter what he said he felt like the words were stupid.

"He was *everything* I had in the world, Phillip."

"You know he was like a brother to me."

"Yeah, I know. That's why I know you gonna do everything it takes to make sure those sons of *bitches* that did this to him get the trip to hell they deserve!"

"Listen, Tania, don't even let those thoughts enter your mind. Jermaine wouldn't want you talking like that."

Lifting her head from his shoulder and folding her arms across her chest she spat out, "Look Phillip, I love you as much as Jermaine did, but don't you *ever* tell me what my husband would and wouldn't want me to be doing! Now are you gonna *kill* those bastards or what?"

Phil-Good kissed her on the forehead and got off the bed. Walking towards the door he turned and looked at her. His heart sank as he looked into her tired face with sympathetic eyes.

"Get some sleep, Tania"

He exited the room, closing the door behind him.

Throwing a glass that sat on the table near the bed against the door it shattered as she yelled out at the top of her lungs. "You son of a bitch! he would do it for you!"

***

Phil-Good returned to his living room. Everyone had pain painted across his or her face. He sunk into his chair. People were broken off into their own little groups talking amongst themselves. Danny, Phil-Fine, and Scripture were all huddled together. Sandra, Carlin, and his wife Charlene sat talking as the record player played The Mississippi Sheiks "Sitting On top Of the World" softly in the background. It played as a soundtrack to this drama they were living through. Conversations continued around him as he blocked out everything and everyone around him. He became entrenched in thought. *They say death come in three's first Rodney Pipe, then Short Stack, now Jermaine.* He would do everything in his power to make sure that it stayed at three. He was dealing with some dishonorable men. They ain't play fair, so he would have to show em what getting dirty was really about.

"Daddy .... Daddy .... Daddy, you alright?" Danny screamed out startling Phil-Good.

Phil-Good snapped back in tune to the people in the room.

"Yeah, yeah, I'm fine, what's up?"

"Nothing, I was asking you if you want me to fix you a plate? I know you ain't ate all day."

"Thank you, son, I'm fine."

Scripture said, "Man, this a lot of shit to happen at one time."

Phil-Good snapped at Scripture, "Watch yo mouth, boy!"

Scripture immediately looked up at Charlene and felt embarrassed for speaking in a profane manner with her present.

"Oh, I apologize, Ms. Charlene."

"Aww, it's okay, honey, it is a lot of shit to happen at one time. That poor girl, Monique didn't even get a chance to mourn her man good, now we are on to the next one. You boys ought to just leave all this foolishness alone and let the streets be."

Carlin spoke up, "Don't start, Charlene."

Charlene rose from her seat and sat in Carlin's lap placing her pointer finger on his lips. "Don't you start. Don't get to messing with my nerves now, Carl."

They continued to ramble on back and forward as Phil-Good made eye contact with Scripture and Danny, signaling them to follow him. As he left the room followed by the two men he said, "Excuse us everyone, I need the boys for a few seconds, please. If everyone hasn't eaten please do so and if you have, eat some more or wrap some up to take with you. I have plenty. It will only go into the garbage."

The three men head back into the den. Phil-Good sat on the edge of his desk as Scripture closed the door behind them.

"Sit down," Phil-Good said, staring at both men with anger in his eyes. They both sat and stared back at him waiting for whatever he had to dish out.

Phil-Good continued, "You two are the last and most important components to help put this thing to bed. Only you two, not Phil-Fine, not, none of ya' soldiers, not Lil-Larry or Boy-Boy—none of them. It's on y'all, I need y'all. Ask yourself now if you got it in you to continue down this road with me 'cause I'm marching right up to the fire and running through it."

"You know I'm with you, Pops," Danny said, staring back at his father stone-faced.

"I got you, Mr. Trenton. Jermaine and cousin Tania took me in, in my time of emergency and you and your organization gave me a job. I'm with you till the end, no matter the outcome."

"Good. Danny, get word to Rusty Bill to set up the meet."

"I'm on it, Pops."

Danny left the room, closing the door behind him. Phil-Good continued, "You do what I asked you to do?"

"Yeah, you were right too. It's no rest for the wicked."

"No doubt, make it clean."

"Anything else, Boss?"

"Yeah, I'll fill you in once Danny gets back to me with a meet-up time and place."

* * *

Monique sat alone on the edge of her bed drinking an Orange Blossom and staring out her bedroom window. She wore her panties, socks, and one of Short Stack's shirts, the one he had on the day before he was murdered. She pulled it from the dirty clothes hamper and put it on. It still had his scent, the smell comforted her soul. She leaned against the wall and closed her eyes. The phone rang. She was hesitant about answering it. She had been receiving calls all week and wanted some time to breathe. On the tenth ring, she opened her eyes, picked up the receiver, and spoke into the phone. "Hello."

"You feel like company?" The familiar voice asked,

She paused for thirty seconds, wondering why she wasn't angry at the question. And wondering if she should be. She spoke in a dry voice, "I'm tired, but I don't want to be alone . . . Larry, the door will be unlocked. Let yourself in and come up to my room."

She hung up the phone before he could respond.

* * *

PUT TO BED

S tanding in the middle of the junkyard, Danny held a powder-white red-nosed pitbull on a leash. Phil-Good sat in a parked car as another car pulled into the junkyard. Phil-Good got out of the car. Wearing a stern expression across his face he grabbed the straps to his cashmere trenchcoat and tightened it around his waist as he approached Ira.

Freddy Fingers and Ira both stepped out of the other car. Freddy Fingers and Danny walked behind Phil-Good and Ira.

Phil-Good lit a cigarette. "You couldn't let bygones be bygones, huh?"

Ira stuck his hands in his pockets. "It's no such thing as forgive and forget in this line of work. You know that better than anybody."

"I suppose."

"What did you call me out here for?"

"I want to come to some common ground where everybody walks away happy. Without any more casualties. By law, I owe you one for Jermaine. You violated the truce and all, but if we can do this without bloodshed, why not try? Besides, if it doesn't work ain't no expiration on death."

"Why come to me? Why not Corelli?"

"Should I have gone with them instead?" Phil-Good asked as he let the cigarette smoke escape through his nose.

"Just asking?"

* * *

In the small town of Elgin, Illinois Charlie Madiassa had been hiding out in a small hotel room. He had stricken a deal with Paul Corelli after he saw that Freddy Fingers was trying to kill him. He knew that someone would try to take him out, but he wasn't sure who it would be. So after paying the bum in the alley fifty dollars to watch his car for him, he ran around the block and crept back up through the alley. He lay down in the alley next to a Dumpster clutching an empty bottle and watching his car. He watched Freddy Fingers blow the back of that old man's head off then blow up the car. He waited until Corelli arrived and told him that Freddy Fingers was responsible for the old man dying, and proof of that was the car bombing. He was trying to silence him before he spoke to them. Paul took him at his word and had him hide out until they thought it was safe to reveal he was still alive. They would deal with Freddy Fingers in their own way. Paul said he had *some detective* on the payroll to deal with it. That's all they told him, they pretty much kept Charlie out of the loop. For this favor though, once Freddy and his uncle were eliminated, he would turn all Madiassa businesses over to the Corelli's and work as a lieutenant. He knew he had sold his soul, but he felt he had no other place to turn.

Charlie placed his key into the lock of his room, turned the doorknob, and then entered. He kicked off his shoes and flopped down on the bed. Lying on the bed with his hands behind his head, his gun holster was still strapped to his frame. His gun clung to the side of his ribcage. He stared up at the ceiling and fell asleep. Within seconds, the quiet room was filled with light snoring. Scripture slid from his hiding spot underneath the bed, quietly. He stood over Charlie as he slept. Gripping a handkerchief doused with his own special concoction of ammonia mixed with lye in his left hand, he gripped Charlie's throat, clutching his Adam's apple. With the other hand containing the handkerchief, he covered his mouth and nose. Charlie's eyes bulged from his face as his chest heaved up and down fighting for oxygen. The handkerchief turned red as he bled from his mouth and nose. His eyes turned bloodshot as they watered and burned from the chemicals. As Scripture felt the final breath escape Charlie's mouth, he squeezed with his left hand and crushed his larynx.

* * *

Danny and Freddy Fingers walked a few paces behind Phil-Good and Ira.

Danny carefully looked Ira over out of the corner of his eye. "I heard about you," he said.

"Is that right?" Ira responded as he stared back through snake eyes with a sinister smirk across his face.

"Yeah, I heard you fingered a guy oh about ten years ago. Surprised you're still *breathing*. Yeah, I had a buddy that was in when you was in. He told me all about you."

"You like to listen to stories, huh?"

"Sometimes, it depends on the source."

"How about fresh from the horse's mouth?"

"I'm listening."

"Now you know I got this name on account of some low-life son of a bitch went around telling everybody I ratted him out."

"Yeah, that much I know."

"And you probably also know that I went away and did five and a half."

"I'm still with you."

"But did you know that *this son of a bitch* they used to call Uncle VD down from Florida had turned states evidence on some of the boys from his home state and got them exiled out the Country?"

"*What the fuck* that got to do with the price of tea in China?"

"I'm getting to it. Like I was saying, he turned state, they relocate him down here. But only somebody recognized him and ratted him out to the outfit."

"*Yeah and?*"

"It would've been an open and shut case. The boys would've taken him for a ride had it come from a reliable source. The guy who recognized him was a *fucking junkie* strung out on that bitch! He was free in the clear, but to really get suspicion off his own ass he threw dirt on my name! And my fucking bad luck, I get pinched the same week with a trunk full of fur coats I lifted from a hijacking I pulled a few weeks before. I get released on a technicality, but the guy I was with did the whole six months!"

"Are you gonna get to the point before *I slit my fucking wrist?*"

"It was all said and done, I mean, *I'm a made fucking guy!* I go way back coming up under my uncles and cousins fresh from Sicily, so my snitching was *fucking* out of the question! But the thing is, everywhere I went people were fucking ragging on me. I'm the fucking butt of everybody's rat jokes. So what I did was I waited and caught this *fucking mutt* coming out of the courthouse one day and shot him in the face on the courthouse steps!"

"In broad daylight?"

"Broad daylight in front of county commissioners and sheriffs. Cause the way I see it, all a man got is his name. And *are you just going to let somebody shit all over your name?* I did my bid and came home. It wasn't nothing I could do about the name, it stuck."

* * *

Scripture drove with the window down mumbling Hail Mary after Hail Mary he had a habit of doing that, it was something he had done for years, it was a reflex reaction after doing a job it helped him to relax he'd been that way since he'd witnessed the murder of a preacher in his home town. Headed back to Chicago to finish the rest of his assignment that Phil-Good had given him, he had completed the first two. One was to follow Detective "Rusty Bill" until he led him to something or someone worthwhile. Once he was led to that hotel and found Charlie alive he knew someday he would cast his dark shadow upon Charlie's doorway. After subconsciously counting seven hundred and seventy-seven Hail Marys, he switched his focus of thought to his next assignment as he entered Chicago's city limits.

* * *

Phil-Good and Ira continued through the junkyard.

"So, you're just gonna give up half of your action?" Ira spoke with sarcasm in his voice.

"Give us a hundred k and your word that you won't try to move in on the rest of the banks we got going and you got a deal," Phil-Good said as he stuck his hand out to shake hands with Ira. Ira stared down at his hand as if it was infected with some incurable disease. Eventually sticking his hand out and taking Phil-Good's in his they both shook firmly.

"I'll have one of my people drop off the money and you can fill him in on the details of the split."

They all walked back to their cars. Freddy Fingers and Ira climbed back into their limousine. Phil-Good and Danny climbed into the other one. They drove off in opposite directions.

* * *

The limousine cruised through traffic. Ira and Freddy Fingers drank whiskey and laughed as they discussed what happened at the meeting.

"Everything go all right?" Freddy Fingers asked.

"Better than I thought," Ira answered.

"Is that a bad thing?" Freddy Fingers asked as he laid his head back and closed his eyes.

"No, it's just that just 'cause you pour shit in coffee and call it *sugar*, that doesn't make it sugar!"

"What you think these boys *clever* enough to try to pull one over on us?"

"I've dealt with these colored boys before and they are anything *but boys!*"

"What then?"

"We play it by ear."

"What about the Corelli's?"

A police siren blared from behind and pulled up behind the car.

The driver pulled over. Freddy Fingers was angered by the fact that some beat cop had the audacity to pull them over. More than half the department was on the payroll, it had to be a dumb rookie. He would give him a piece of his mind.

"What the fuck is this?" Freddy Fingers blurted out.

"Be cool, it's nothing." Ira spat out, slightly annoyed.

Detective Rusty Bill approached the driver's window. "Do you have license and registration?"

"Yes sir." The driver handed him his license and registration.

"I'll be right back." He walked back to his car and radioed headquarters.

Freddy Fingers grew agitated and nervous. He pulled his gun and laid it on his lap. "I got a bad feeling about this shit."

"What are you doing? Put that fucking thing away!"

Rusty Bill returned. "You mind stepping out of the car?" he asked.

"What's the problem officer?" The driver asked with an attitude staring into Rusty Bill's eyes with arrogance.

"No problem, step out of the car please." Rusty Bill stepped back tapping the butt of his firearm with his index finger.

The driver, not wanting to argue or prolong the situation stepped out of the car. Freddy Fingers sat impatiently tapping a foot, his hand against his thigh. With his head hanging out of the window he spat at the officer.

"What the fuck is the deal, flat foot?"

Rusty Bill now upset snapped back at Freddy Fingers, waiving his gun angrily his lips curled as he spoke through clenched teeth. "Hey you, fucking sit there till I tell you to move!"

"See what the fuck I mean?" Freddy Fingers barked at Ira.

Rusty Bill was at his boiling point with Freddy Fingers' blatant disrespect for his badge. "You gentlemen want to step out of the car for me, please?"

Ira stepped out of the car. Upset that this had taken up more time than he felt it should, he'd lost his patience also. "Do you know who the *fuck* I am?" he bellowed at Rusty Bill.

Rusty Bill knew exactly who he was. Paul Corelli had paid handsomely to have him put on ice, him and Freddy Fingers.

The detective responded with a smirk, "Yes sir, I do."

"I'm sure we can work this all out without incident?"

Two more squad cars pulled up coming from both directions.

"I'm sorry, sir, but can you put your hands on top of your head?" Rusty Bill pulled out his gun and had it trained on Ira.

Ira placed his hands on top of his head. Inside the car, Freddy Fingers cocked back the hammer to his gun. The officers got out of their cars and had their guns drawn. The officers yelled for Freddy Fingers to get out of the car. One of the officers' rushed over to Rusty Bill and attempted to put handcuffs on Ira a shot is fired, hitting the officer in the chest. His heavy frame merged with the passenger door of the car as he crashed into it and began bleeding from the mouth. Rusty Bill took cover and began firing at Ira. It was unclear who shot first, but that was just the excuse Freddy Fingers was waiting for. He jumped out of the car firing, hitting one of the officers in the chest. Ira began running and pulling out his gun and firing at the other officers as he made his attempt to escape. The officers all took fire hitting the driver multiple times in the back as he tried to escape.

Freddy Fingers was on Ira's heels, taking up the rear, and firing back in their attempt to get away alive. He'd lost his grip on reality. Hysterical laughter escaped from his mouth like a lunatic as the officers dropped like flies from the damage he caused from his .45 caliber automatic he wielded with precision. He picked off two officers. Was headed for his third when he was hit twice simultaneously, once in the back of the head and once in the forehead! It was unsure what shot killed him, but it didn't matter. He was dead before he hit the ground. His head exploded into a pile of bloody flesh on the cement.

Ira was surrounded. He threw down his gun and lay down on the ground. The area was swarming with police, kicking and punching Ira as they put on the cuffs! Rusty Bill walked over and got the men off Ira. He shoved him in the rear of the car and slammed the door closed. He headed back towards his car. He wanted him dead, but there were too many witnesses. Paul would just have to settle for one dead and the other sentenced for multiple murders. Across the street on the roof, Scripture dropped the rifle with the telescope attached. He had sent off the initial shot that killed the first officer! He climbed down to the street where Phil-Good and Danny were waiting in a parked car. He got in as the car jerked off into traffic.

* * *

Phil-Good popped the cork on the champagne bottle. They held a private celebration at The Diamond Deluxe. The Crew was all there, all except Scripture, which wasn't a big surprise. He never really partied with them; he mostly stayed to himself. Phil-Good held up his glass in a toast.

"I told you, son, do like I say and everything was gonna be all right."

"I'll never question you again, Pops," Danny said as he ran his fingers through his goatee.

"You won't have to."

"What you mean, Pops?"

"I'm done, I'm too old for this shit."

"What you talking about *too old*, you're still a lot smarter than these niggas out here."

"Yeah, I know. That's why I'm getting out while I can and enjoy some of this money."

Phil-Fine walked over to Phil-Good and kissed him on the forehead.

"Well, I'm glad, Pops."

Danny downed his glass of champagne. "Me too."

"It's all on you, son. I'm leaving it with a clean slate, no beefs with nobody. But I'm always here if you need advice."

"What about the Corelli's?"

"I just told you, listen to me and you'll be alright. When I say a clean slate, I mean a clean slate."

* * *

At that very moment, on the other side of town, Scripture stood staring out of a ninth-floor hotel room window for what had to be fifteen minutes. He stared across the street into an open window of a hotel room clutching a bow and arrow. He was on his seven-hundred-seventy-sixth Hail Mary when he paused and took an easy breath. He whispered, "*Hail Mary, full of grace, the Lord is with thee; blessed art thou amongst women, and blessed is the fruit of thy womb, Jesus. Holy Mary, Mother of God, pray for us sinners now and at the hour of our death. Amen!*"

Releasing the arrow, it speared across the street through the air into the other room landing in Paul Corelli's throat. He fell back on the coffee table. He was dead before his men knew what happened. Scripture put the bow and reaming arrows back into his bag, exited the hotel through the back entrance, and drove quietly away from the scene.

* * *

ADAPTATION

D anny, Phil-Fine, Scripture, and Randy all sat at the group's private table in the back of The Diamond Deluxe drinking and discussing their next power moves. The Diamond Deluxe was nothing compared to The Palm in its heyday. Long gone were the live bands and open gambling. They had to resort to jukebox machines and private gambling rooms hidden away in the basements of the two flat buildings they owned.

"I don't know, I mean shit ain't how it used to be. It's a new day. The world's changing. It's 1952. People hardly play numbers with us no more they are all scared so they play with that Irish fuck, O'Reily. I can't really fight. Ain't no more Big Six." Danny said as he stretched his legs standing behind his large oak desk.

"You make it sound like you ready to lay down and *die*," Randy said as he playfully began to slap boxing with Danny throwing soft jabs to his ribcage.

"Naw, it's not that. It's that these niggas are *scared*. I mean they don't make men like my pops no more!" Danny replied biting down on his bottom lip as he tried blocking some of the jabs Randy threw and throwing some back himself.

"Hell naw. Jermaine, Short Stack, and Rodney Pipe. It seems like all the *real* niggas are dead!" Randy said laughing as he and Danny slapped hands and hugged.

"Hell yeah, shit except us. Shit, it's like, it's like, we are the last of a dying breed and shit! That bitch, Johansen ran damn near all of my numbers operations into the ground! I don't even know why I'm still paying these cops and shit. They ain't no good without city officials."

"It'll get greater later," Randy said as he flopped down into his chair across from Danny propping his feet up on the desk.

"Aint that the fucking truth! If I ain't got shit, I got patience. Something gonna give." Danny said as he sat at his desk and folded his hands.

"Well, something better gives soon, 'cause if it don't we all gonna starve to death!" Scripture said speaking for the first time.

"All right fellas, we moving in a whole new direction then. Supply and demand changed. Gambling is all but dead, at least for us anyway. Our new bread and butter gonna be narcotics." Danny wore a sinister smirk across his face as the words escaped his mouth. He removed a bag of weed from his desk drawer and tobacco papers setting them on the desk.

"What we are going move, smack?" Randy asked staring through quizzical eyes.

"Yeah, I got a good connect on the West Coast."

"I don't know shit about no *fucking* heroin."

"All you need to know is don't ever try that *shit* and we going make money hand over fist!"

Scripture asked, "Where do I fit in, in all of this?" As he sat on the edge of the desk.

"Your position stays the same. We gonna still need to put motherfuckers on ice!"

"What about O'Reily?"

"What about 'em? Fuck 'em! What do you think he got a copyright on the drug trade?"

Randy says. "You know this might spell death for all of us?"

"Don't you start getting soft on me now!"

"Ain't nobody getting soft. All I'm saying is we can't be doing stupid shit!"

"What, I'm stupid now? Huh? You saying I'm leading us in the wrong direction or some shit?"

"Nall I ain't saying none of that it's just that..."

Danny interrupts. "Look I don't need nobody second-guessing what we trying to do. Either you're down or you're not. 'Cause shit, nigga, you replaceable!"

"Aww, it's like *that?*"

"I don't see it being no other way."

"Let me go outside before I say some shit I can't take back."

"Yeah, that would be your best bet!"

Randy jumped up and stormed out of the lounge.

* * *

Kenneth O' Reily was the new boss of Windy City. It all seemed to happen out of nowhere. Kenneth O'Reily was putting in work and making political connections. Not to say that the Irish had a complete run of the city, but they had a big piece of the pie. Kenneth O'Reily was a third generation born in the States from people that migrated from Ireland. Not to mention third-generation poor white trash. He had made it to where his father and grandfather could have only dreamed. Boss of a family over men who were bosses of their own families! He wasn't educated and spoke with a foul demeanor, ineloquent in matters of diplomacy. He ruled his criminal empire with an iron fist. Standing six feet even and weighing two hundred fifty pounds with red hair and a thick red mustache, he spoke with a heavy Irish accent. He and Ice Pick Iyoki, who had long become O'Reily's unofficial right-hand man. To those in the public's eye, Ice Pick was merely a hitman for hire. A kill-on-demand mob man lackey. However, the truth is most of O'Reily's major moves came from the maneuvering and strategic mind of Ice Pick Iyoki. They might seem a strange pair, but they got the job done.

A thirty-two-year-old Mongolian standing at five-feet-four inches and weighing one-hundred seventy-five pounds. He came to Chicago five years before on the run from Hong Kong authorities. Wanted for multiple murders of key Triad members. O'Reilly paid a half-a-million-dollar fee to the Triads to spare his life. Ice Pick is unable to return to his Native country, or work for the Triads of the states. He pledged his allegiance to O'Reily and his family.

Kenneth O'Reily and Ice Pick Iyoki both sat in O'Reily's hotel suite talking with a scraggly-looking old-timer.

O'Reily crushed the crackers into a bowl of soup. "You're sure it was a big falling out?"

The old timer responds, "Yeah I'm sure. Right in the middle of The Diamond Deluxe, he told him he was easy to replace."

"Is that all that was said?"

"Yes sir, after that Randy stormed out."

O'Reily reached into his pocket and pulled out a few bills and handed it to the man.

"If you hear anything else, give me a call."

The old timer took the money. "Yes sir, Mr. O'Reily I'll do just that, sir."

As he left the room, Ice Pick Iyoki stood.

"You think we can flip him, boss?"

"In America, loyalty and betrayal walk a thin line and either can be bought for the right price. Go proposition him, see where his head is."

* * *

Danny had been more right than he might have realized. His new venture had turned out greater than he had ever imagined. Sitting in his new office over at the new sanitation company he had built from the ground up, talking with Scripture about the next move to be made.

"I told you, I told your ass we were going make more money in a month than we did in a year running numbers," Danny said.

Stretched out on the leather couch clutching a handful of hundred dollar bills in one hand and two more rubberbands bundled together of all hundred dollar bills laying in his lap. Scripture laughed aloud. He had to agree they had made a lot of fucking money real fucking fast. "Yeah, I see now. You got garbage trucks and shit."

"Man, it's a bitch trying to get these government contracts and shit. If I can get my hands on public school contracts, then we talking 'bout some shit."

The telephone rang and Danny picked it up. "Hello," he answered.

A voice on the other end of the telephone is Ice Pick Iyoki. "You have two days to hand over your contracts or else!"

Danny became heated but tried not to let it show. His lips became twisted as he attempted to talk with a calm voice. "*What?* Who the fuck is this playing on my phone?"

Ice Pick Iyoki hung up leaving Danny listening to a dial tone.

"Hello, hello!" Danny yelled and then slammed down the telephone.

Scripture looked concerned. "What was that about?" he asked, standing from the couch and stretching.

Danny still sat with his face twisted. "I don't know the *mother* hung up, talking 'bout giving up my contracts or else. Damn, don't nobody want to see a nigga get paid!"

* * *

FUCKED AND BAMBOOZLED!

Randy was coming out of The Diamond Deluxe when a car jumped up on the sidewalk blocking his path. Ice Pick Iyoki jumped out pointing a gun. Although Randy had never met Ice Pick before, he knew who he was. It wasn't like the city was crawling with Chinese gangsters and it sure the fuck were no fucking Chinese on the police force. The move hadn't fazed Randy at all. He had guns in his face before.

"What the *fuck* you want, chink motherfucker?"

Ice Pick didn't flinch at being called the racial slur. He was used to it. He had heard it all before chink, slanted eyes, rice eater, gook. They were all the same, but he usually heard it right before he pulled the trigger and blew they shit all over the cement.

Ice Pick Iyoki says, *"Just get the fuck in the car!"*

Randy, interested in what he had to say climbed into the back of the car. After they both got inside, the car pulled off.

"Can I put this away? I want to talk?" Ice Pick Iyoki said, gesturing toward the gun he still had trained on Randy.

Randy leaned back and got comfortable. "Talk motherfucker."

Ice Pick Iyoki put his gun back in his holster and pointed toward a bottle of brandy. "Would you like a drink?"

Randy, not really being the sociable kind, especially after being drawn on got straight to the point. "Naw man, talk to me about what the fuck you want and let me move on."

Ice Pick Iyoki noticed the vibe. "Do you know who I am?"

Randy lit a cigarette and smiled. "Ice Pick Iyoki, O'Reily's Chinese golden boy."

Ice Pick smiled, aware that his reputation had merit of its own. "I hear you are not happy with the direction things are going with Trenton."

Randy, trying not to display any emotion one way or another, although he was confused about where he would get information like that from, answered back nonchalantly. "If I am or I ain't, that ain't none of your business, rice boy."

Ice Pick's words were dripping with confidence. "Let's say I make it my business and make it worthwhile for everybody involved."

"I'm listening."

Ice Pick continued, "Let's say you come work for Mr. O'Reily. A man of your talents shouldn't waste them by being humiliated in public."

"I don't know. What kind of man would I be by turning my back on Danny? Shit, I would think my trust with y'all would be thin."

"Don't put so much emphasis on trust. Do the job that you're paid to do and we will pay you. It's a job, not a marriage."

"What are we talking about for pay?"

"Let's say double whatever you're getting."

Randy's eyes lit up with excitement 'cause he knew he was being offered the opportunity to write his own ticket. "What I got to do?"

Ice Pick, feeling as though he had snagged the prize answered, "Hand over the remaining banks Trenton's got and tell us everything about his heroin operation."

Randy, faking as though he was surprised said, "Yall don't miss a beat, huh?" But he knew that they knew about the operation. Everybody in the city knew; it was common knowledge.

"We can't afford not to. Do we have a deal?"

Randy smiled. "It sounds like a deal to me."

The car pulled over and Randy got out rubbing his hands together as he watched the car jet from the curb.

* * *

Later that night after processing everything that had gone on earlier that day, Randy knew what he had to do. He would have to be precise if he wanted everything to go over right 'cause he wouldn't get a second chance.

He walked into The Diamond Deluxe. Danny and Scripture were having drinks.

Danny was excited to see his old friend. Danny motioned toward Randy. "Come on over here and have a drink with me."

Randy with a forced smile made his way across the room to where Danny and Scripture were seated. "What's going on?"

Danny poured Randy a drink of scotch and poured himself another drink. Randy downed the drink in one gulp. "Thanks, man."

Danny had been thinking about Randy right before he had walked through the door. They had been through a lot together, street fights, wars with the Italians, and the government. Fucked a lot of fine women together and made a lot of fucking money. He felt ashamed that they had never once in their twenty-plus years of knowing one another argued in front of anybody. It was bad for business, even if it was just the crew around; they didn't do it.

Danny smiled. "Not a problem. You know that whole thing the other day? I was way out of line. You my right-hand man. I should've never come at you like that. I'm sorry."

Randy was glad that he had been the better man that he knew he was. Was glad that Danny had stepped up to the plate and apologized.

"It ain't nothing, man. In fact, I was thinking you should let me get full run of the policy stations so you can concentrate more on the other ventures you got going."

Danny had already felt like selling the rest of the banks anyway. This was right on time. "Shit, why not? Kick me back a portion and it's yours."

"Let's have a toast. To new beginnings." Danny said with a proud smile across his face.

Scripture grabbed the bottle of scotch and filled the three glasses on the table. They all lifted their glasses.

Randy stared off into space with a triumphant smile. "To new beginnings."

* * *

Ice Pick Iyoki sat in Kenneth O'Reily's hotel room eating breakfast, his usual, a bowl of steamed white rice, three pieces of bacon, and three eggs sunny side up. As he cut into the egg with his fork, the yolk ran on the side of his plate. He sopped it up with a slice of bread. The telephone rang, disturbing his meal. He picked up the telephone.

"Hello," he answered.

"It's done," Randy said.

"Good. Bring the money down to Mr. O'Reily's hotel suite. I have a special project for you."

He slammed down the telephone and continued eating his breakfast. Not even ten minutes later, Randy walked into the hotel carrying an attaché case filled with money from the day's take of the numbers racket. Little did he know Scripture had followed him!

* * *

Danny laid in bed with his wife, Apricot when the phone rings. By the ninth ring, he realized Apricot wasn't getting up and the asshole on the other end wasn't hanging up. He picked up the telephone.

"What!" he yelled through the receiver.

Scripture said, "We need you down here at the sanitation company."

Danny was still not quite awake. "What? Man, it's seven o'clock in the morning."

Scripture continued, "Two of the drivers got dragged out of their trucks and *beat* half to death!"

Danny, now more alert wipes the cold from his eyes. "Man, *what* are you talking about?"

"It was a message from O' Reily to hand over those contracts."

Danny, thinking to himself if it ain't one thang it's a muthafucking 'nother! "I'm on my way!"

"*Danny.*"

"Yeah!" Danny yelled through the telephone more out of habit than out of truly being upset.

"They say it was two guys that beat them up. Ice Pick Iyoki and yo' boy, Randy."

Danny had reached his boiling point. "Fuck it, man. I'll be there in an hour."

An hour later, after taking a shit, shower, and shave, Danny was dressed and at the sanitation company and talking with Phil-Fine and Scripture. Danny was hurt by Randy's actions. He had a cut of everything Danny had, damn near more so than his own brother. This move Randy had made was dangerous. Danny knew before it was all over, blood would be shed.

Phil-Fine said, "What's the plan, man?"

"We got to be smart about this. Scripture sends out a message."

"What kind of message?"

Danny leaned back in his chair and propped his feet up on his desk. "One that will get O'Reily's attention."

"*Then one of the twelve called Judas Iscariot went to the chief priests and said, What are you to give me if I deliver him to you? And they counted out thirty pieces of silver. So from that time, he sought the opportunity to betray Him!* How much do you think Randy got for you?" Scripture spat out, a cunning smile escaped his lips.

Phil-Fine's eyes squinted as his lips curled angrily. "What about Randy?"

Danny's face turned to anger when he heard Randy's name. "Let me worry about Randy."

* * *

The living room was dark as Ice Pick Iyoki entered his home and locked the door behind himself. When he turned on the light his heart dropped to find Scripture sitting in a chair in his living room pointing a gun.

Scripture knew he had the drop on him, but he didn't take anything for granted. Scripture waved the gun nonchalantly. "Be easy there, china boy."

Ice Pick thought he might have a chance to talk his way out of death and raised his arms. "Can I at least fix myself a drink?"

Scripture had heard it all before, but he wondered what angle he would come with. He nodded his head.

"Go 'head, be easy about it."

Ice Pick took off his coat and laid it across a nearby chair. He walked over to the bar and began pouring a drink. "What can I do for you?"

A poor attempt to control the situation, Scripture thought. "What makes you think it's anything you can do?"

Ice Pick was far from being a timid man, he always spoke his mind. "I don't care what people say, I don't think you're *all* animals."

Scripture not giving a fuck what he thought one way or the other replied, "Is that right?"

Ice Pick continued, "I'm sure every man has his price."

Scripture was still not amused. "You think so, huh?"

Ice Pick felt as though he almost had him on the hook and went in for the kill. "Yes, I do. I mean, that's why we're in this right? Money, power, respect. Everybody got a price. What's yours?"

Scripture figured he would humor him. "What about justice?"

"Justice doesn't get the bills paid."

Scripture thought, *There it is, the money route. All niggas would sell their own mama for the right price.* The shit was an insult, but Scripture had heard it all before. The shit made him laugh on the inside. The last words of a condemned man often did.

"Yeah, but it feels good!"

Ice Pick still felt that he could appeal to the man's lust for money. "Who are we to pass judgment and issue out *justice* as we see fit?"

"As God lives, who has taken away my justice, and the almighty, who has made my soul bitter, As long as my breath is in me, and the breath of God in my nostrils, My lips will not speak wickedness, Nor my tongue utter deceit. Far be it from me that I should say you are right; Till I die I will not put away my integrity from me. My righteousness I hold fast, and will not let it go; my heart shall not reproach me as long as I live. May my enemy be like the wicked, and he who rises up against me like the unrighteous. For what is the hope of the hypocrite, Though he may gain much If God takes away his life? Will God hear his cry when trouble comes upon him? Huh, China boy? Will *God* hear your cry?"

Ice Pick Iyoki had heard of urban wise tales of a Scripture quoting hit man. By hearing those words he knew that he could talk from now on until the Second Coming and this man would never change his mind. He threw the empty glass, missing Scripture.

"You self-righteous son a bitch..." he yelled out.

The words barely escaped his mouth as Scripture pulled the trigger. Hit twice in the stomach, Ice Pick Iyoki died with his eyes open.

* * *

Kenneth O'Reily was sitting in his hotel room getting dressed. He was expected for dinner with the Mayor.

Randy rushed in. "I got bad news, boss."

O'Reily was not paying any particular attention to Randy.

"What is it? Where in the hell is Ice Pick?"

"They found Ice Pick Iyoki this morning, *dead*! One of his feet was cut off and stuffed in his mouth!"

O'Reily could not hide the look of hurt that covered his face.

"What kind of *sick fucks* would dismember a man being sent over to the other side? Unholy niggers they are!"

"You think it was Danny, too, huh?"

"Right you are, and I'm suspecting they'll be gunning for you next." Randy came across as overly arrogant.

"Shid, them niggas know I aint's to be trifled with. I can handle myself, boss. You the one I'm worried about."

"Why is that laddie?" O'Reily asked not believing him.

"Danny plays for keeps, he is far from dumb. He knows the laws of nature."

O'Reily looked confused. "I'm sorry, I don't follow."

"He knows if you kill the head the body must *die!*"

O'Reily was now hanging on his every word. "He wouldn't be foolish enough to come up against me head-on."

Randy smiled a devilish smile. "He already has. What do you think hitting Ice Pick Iyoki was? You should let me meet with him, and see if we can't settle this without more bloodshed."

"Go ahead, but I want nothing less than him coming in with us and splitting all of his operations fifty/fifty and he takes twenty percent of all of my operations."

"Right boss, I'll get on it right now."

"How do you know he won't shoot you in the face on contact?"

Randy still paraded about with his overconfident swagger. "Business is business, and Danny always puts business above personal beefs. We go way back, I know this man better than he knows himself."

As Randy exited from the room, O'Reily continued tying his bow tie and picked up the telephone. "Hello, operator, get me Wilma O'Reily in New Jersey ... Hello how are you doing, Aunt Wilma ... yeah the kids are fine. Is Vincent around ... Vinnie, I need a favor."

* * *

Phil-Good sat on his yacht off the coast of Mexico, wearing a straw hat to cover his face from the sun. He wore a yellow and orange short-sleeved Hawaiian-looking shirt covered with palm trees and flamingos, a pair of beige shorts, and leather sandals. It had been many years since he had stepped away from the game. This was how he spent his time now, fishing and sitting in the sun. He felt a cool breeze blow across his face.

Ilene, his companion for the weeklong trip came up from the galley carrying a pitcher of chilled pineapple juice mixed with vodka. She sat the pitcher on the table next to a bowl of fresh fruit she had sliced. Phil-Good's favorites were pineapple, kiwi, and watermelon. He smiled at the thirty-something-year-old woman as she picked up a piece of the pineapple and sucked the juice from the fruit. She spit the pineapple into the water after no more juice was left to suck.

She dropped down to her knees and removed Phil-Good's tool from his shorts. She licked the tip of his genital. His legs shook as he tried to remain calm. Still holding his grip on the fishing pole, he finally drops it to his side as Ilene pulls his entire dick into her mouth. As he felt the warmth from her jaws, he poured himself a drink of the sweet alcohol. He leaned back, closed his eyes, and sipped his drink through a straw. Ilene looked up at Phil-Good, who was still sitting with his eyes closed with a weird smile on his face.

It was obvious he was enjoying the wonderful job she was doing. It made her feel good that she was doing a good job. She stopped and smiled. Phil-Good grabbed the back of her head and pushed her face back to his throbbing manhood. Ilene went back at it this time even more passionately. Ten minutes later, Phil-Good's eyes rolled to the back of his head. His heart rate sped up, and his legs began to twitch. Ilene felt he was about to come, so she sucked harder and faster as the thick fluid rushed into her mouth. She almost choked as she closed her eyes and swallowed.

Phil-Good let out a high-pitched scream and lay back with his eyes closed completely frozen. Ilene stood laughing as she wiped her mouth from a job well done. She set the towel on the table next to the pitcher of liquor and sat on Phil-Good's lap, brushing her hair from her face and giggling.

"It was that good, huh? Too tired to even hold me?"

Phil-Good didn't respond. In fact, he never even budged when she sat on his lap. She stopped smiling and looked down into Phil-Good's face.

His expression was blank as if he wasn't even there. She reached down and grabbed his hand he never opened his eyes.

"*Baby.*"

No response. Ilene let go of his hand. It dropped heavy on his side like dead weight. That's when Ilene knew, in that quick moment of heated passion . . . *Phil-Good was gone!*

* * *

It was all set. At least in his mind, it was. Randy had everyone in a position exactly where he needed them to be for this thing to go off right. He was pulling up to a red light at the corner of East 47th Street when a car pulled up to him and the passenger jumped out and reached through his window. Before he could pull it off, he was cut across the face underneath his eye down to his chin with a straight razor! He fell back in his seat screaming in pain as he smashed down on the gas and crashed into an elderly couple driving when he went through the red light.

The man who cut him was Scripture. Randy knew this much because he had seen his face. Scripture had walked over to him with the razor still dripping blood and fragments of Randy's facial skin on the blade.

Scripture yanked open the door. "You only breathing because of Danny 'cause if it was up to me, I would've cut you from *ear to ear!*"

Randy felt the open air hitting his new wound as blood ran into his ear and mouth. He never even attempted to draw his weapon. He just looked at Scripture with sincerity in his eyes.

"I was on my way to see Danny and Phil-Fine to clear the bad blood."

Scripture walked back to his car and drove off.

* * *

Randy had checked himself out of the hospital after he got his stitches, well over a hundred. He had word that the meet would go down now. He had twenty minutes to get over to the Golden Lady. He had telephoned O'Reily and told him to meet them there. Randy thought it was still a chance he could pull it off and come out alive!

* * *

A stranger sat in the Diamond Deluxe talking to the bartender. The bartender was the same scraggly old man who had been giving O'Reily and Ice Pick Iyoki inside information on the Trenton Crew. He had been working for O'Reily for the past six months gathering information. The stranger was a well-dressed well-spoken colored man in his early twenties and only spoke when he felt it necessary. The truth of the matter is Kenneth O'Reily had a man fly in just for this meeting as a form of insurance.

The Stranger sipped his drink.

"Which one is Danny?"

The scraggly old man motioned with his eyes. "That's him at the table in the far corner. Him and his little brother, Phil-Fine."

The stranger, not wanting to cause attention does not turn to look. He looked up into the mirror behind the bar and spotted them through the reflection.

"What about this Scripture I keep hearing about?"

"He ain't here yet, I'm surprised. Knowing what's going down, I thought he'd be here by now." The bartender answered as he stuffed peanuts from the bar into his mouth.

"It doesn't matter, long as I get the Trenton boys and Randy. Where is he at?"

"Beats me. Probably going to come in with Mr. O'Reily."

* * *

Danny and Phil-Fine sat at the table trying to relax. They had popped their second bottle of champagne.

Danny said, "Everybody know what they supposed to be doing?"

"Yeah, we straight. You not nervous, are you?"

Danny answered with an air of arrogance, "Man, hell naw. You know I live for this *kind of* shit."

Randy and Kenneth O'Reily walked into The Diamond Deluxe and joined Danny and Phil-Fine at the table.

Randy said, "Sorry about your pops?"

Danny and Phil-Fine both ignored Randy's remark.

Phil-Fine gestured towards Randy. "We got to pat you down, man."

"Hold on, man. This ain't even called for. Everybody here knows I'm holding."

Phil-Fine didn't budge on what he had just said. "We'll give your piece back when you leave."

Randy knew that it had gone too far, but he was still hurt. "Danny, man, I thought we were better than this?"

"It ain't personal. You know how it is."

Randy reached into his suit pocket, pulled out his gun, and handed it to Phil-Fine. "Yeah, I know."

O'Reily said, "If you think that's what I came here for, you are sadly mistaken. The only way you get my gun is off my *cold, dead body!*"

Danny started laughing. "Be careful what you wish for. No, I'm kidding. Come on sit down, sit down. What can I do for you, Mr. O'Reily?"

O'Reily sat down with his back facing the wall. He leaned back in his chair.

"Randy here tells me you were interested in merging our two operations for the greater good."

Phil-Fine with a stone face replied, "The greater good of who?"

"Why everybody involved, of course."

Danny said, "Of course, but what are we talking about for numbers?"

Randy, doing his best impression of a good Uncle Tom jumped right in. "Now I told Mr. O'Reily here that fifty/fifty of yours and not of his wasn't fair so ..."

O'Reily cut him off, "So I thought more along the lines of fifty/fifty yours and sixty/forty of mine."

Danny did not smile; he did not frown either. In fact, the look on his face was indistinguishable. "That is a handsome offer, but I was thinking more along the lines of I keep a hundred percent of mine and let you keep a hundred percent of yours, that way *everybody is happy!*"

O'Reily's entire face turned red. "See lad, that's where you're wrong, 'cause that still leaves me unhappy."

Phil-Fine unable to mask his frustration said, "*Well, you can't make everybody happy all of the time.*"

Randy smiled. "Wait a minute, Danny, I thought that."

Danny's emotions were now in full view as he exploded in anger. "You thought what? you back-stabbing son of a bitch!"

Randy tried to diffuse the situation. "Whoa! Whoa Danny, man. We had a deal."

Danny still yelled, "What? A *deal* like you made with Mr. O'Reily here?"

The hired hitman still sat at the bar watching and waiting for his opportunity to do what he was hired for.

O' Reily tried to take control of the situation and spoke in a calm, cool voice. "Whatever you're thinking about, lad, forget about it. It won't work. I thought of it a hundred times over and re-thought it over backward, a hundred times more!"

Danny composed himself. "You're right. You are a smart man. I'll give you that. *But how are your eyes?*"

O'Reily looked confused. "I'm sorry, I don't follow?"

"Your eyes, you *Irish cracker*. In the far corner. The white boy with the black chick on his lap."

O'Reily turns to see a beautiful woman in a short skirt and a silk see-through blouse sitting on a white man's lap. As they both laughed, the woman stuck her tongue in the man's mouth, kissing him. She pulled back smiling and slit his throat. His head slumped to the side as his blood splattered the walls.

Danny didn't flinch. "The other side of the room; the colored fellow standing near the john."

O'Reily turned facing the tall lanky man standing near the bathroom smoking a cigarette. Before O'Reily blinked, the man was snatched into the bathroom from behind. Only seconds later, Scripture exited, wiping blood from a knife on a white handkerchief.

Danny didn't skip a beat as he continued, "You follow me now?"

O'Reily tried to mask his shock with a light smile. "Not exactly. What? Are they *supposed* to be with me?"

Phil-Fine's smirked devilishly. "Oh, now you want to talk to *us* directly?"

O'Reily was now becoming upset. "Are you gonna keep talking in circles or fucking come out with it?"

Scripture returned holding the scraggly old man by the neck.

O'Reily says. "What's this?"

Danny looked at him with a cocky expression. "What? You thought we ain't know about this piece of shit?"

O'Reily was doing a horrible job at trying to convince the men that he didn't know the man. "It doesn't matter what you think you know 'cause we all know if you touch me, my family is gonna bring down *hell* on you niggers in biblical proportions."

Danny smiled. "Scripture!"

"*Vengeance is mine says the Lord!*"

Danny looked disappointed. "*Vengeance is mine?* Man, I know that one."

Scripture shrugged his shoulders. "Sorry, I went blank."

Before the words left his mouth good, he snapped the old man's neck. The room filled with the smell of shit. The old man had released all of his bodily functions.

Scripture dragged the body to the bathroom and returned.

Danny walked over to Randy. "See, from day one when this piece of shit here pulled your coat to me and Randy falling out I been on to you."

O'Reily sat silently trying not to look dumbfounded. "Well, what's with all the games?"

Danny took his time weaving his tale. "You ever play chess, Mr. O'Reily?"

O'Reily figured he would humor them 'cause shit, he was going to win in the end anyway. "More of a checkers man myself."

Danny walked around the room. "Oh, that's a shame. You strike me as a chess man. It's a *thinking* man's game, you know?"

O'Reily tapped his glass with his fingernail, tapping his foot underneath the table impatiently. "I never had the patience."

"That's too bad, but you get the gist of the game, right?"

"Try to checkmate the other guy's King, right?"

Danny smiled "Basically, but you have to be *strategic*, you know military-minded."

O'Reily with a smug look across his face said, "You *think* you got all the angles covered, huh?"

Danny shrugged his shoulders, raising his left eyebrow. "*I don't know, do I?* Don't answer that. Let's see. First, you planted this piece of shit in my bar. Then, you had that chink fuck kidnap this piece of shit right here and turn him against us, right? Don't answer that. Set up this bogus meeting and planted hit men all over the room, but the thing I don't get is why hire local people? You had to know I would finger them the second they came in."

O'Reily poured himself a drink. "Maybe you're too smart for your own good? I told you everything you thought of I already thought of."

Danny stopped pacing, looked at O'Reily, and held up his pointer finger. "But what about this game I was talking about?"

"What game? *Chess*, you think this is like some *silly* game? I give you credit though, you are smart, but not smart enough. Anybody who knows me will tell you I *always* have an ace in the hole!"

Danny sat down across from O'Reily. "I don't mean to cut you off, but I didn't tell you the other aspect of the game."

O'Reily no longer tried to mask his impatience. "And that is!"

Danny looked into his eyes. "*Sacrifice!*" he spoke in an almost a whisper

"Sacrifice of what?"

Danny drank out of the bottle of whiskey. "The other part of the game is sacrifice. You see they have these pieces called ponds and the ponds are foot soldiers that would be our friend Scripture drug into the bathroom. And Randy here. But only you don't always sacrifice the ponds sometimes you use them as bait."

"I don't follow!"

Phil-Fine also looked confused. "*Me either!*" he said.

Danny, in total control of the situation, smirked at the men. "I'm not surprised, little brother. See, to make this thing come across authentic I couldn't let you in on it."

Randy was eager to join in the fun. He cut him off. "Danny, may I?"

Danny, with a face of stone, bowed his head toward Randy. "Be my guest."

Randy licked his lips. "See, right after Iyoki snatched me off the streets and let me go, I pulled Danny's coat and we started watching everybody who worked at The Diamond Deluxe till we saw who the rat was."

Phil-Fine smiled. "Hold on. How you know me or Scripture wasn't gonna off Randy just on GP?"

Randy rubbed his new scar. "We didn't!"

Danny cut him off. "It was a chance we had to take."

Randy couldn't help being pissed about his face, but he couldn't blame Scripture. He would've done worse if he were in his shoes. He hated traitors.

Randy continued, "By the way I'm *sho' the fuck* glad y'all ain't try!"

Phil-Fine was laughing at the clever scheme. "All that was genius!"

Danny still seated took a mocking bow. "Thank you!"

O'Reily begins to clap in mock approval. "Bravo, great fucking performance, but excuse me if I must take the stage myself for the grand finale!"

Danny leaned back in his seat. "Oh, by all means, be my guest. *Aw man,* how did I forget the best part? Do you know Ms. Angel Bedford?"

O'Reily, now anxious to get this whole circus over with eyes the hired hit man still sitting at the bar. They were *so smart* but they were *so dumb!* "No, I do not. What the fuck do that got to do with anything?"

"Nothing except that Ms. Angel Bedford works as a telephone operator over at the hotel where you live. She pulled our coat to a certain out-of-town guest you had flown in just for little old me."

O'Reily looked shocked. "What if I did? Even if you do kill me, it's too late now. He's been paid. He'll finish the job if I'm alive or not!"

Danny expression intentionally came across his face as smug. "You think so?"

O'Reily was feeling as though the ball was in his court. "You bet your *black* ass. He's a fucking professional, best on the East Coast!"

"A colored man? You surprise me, O'Reily. What would you say if I said you wasted your money? He was already taken care of."

O'Reily thought -an obvious bluff. They were smart, but they weren't quick enough. They would all be dead before the night was over. He humored them. "I would say you were full of *shit.* Taken care of how?"

"One of my guys spotted him and put him on ice."

O'Reily spoke with an air of confidence. "I would know for a fact you were full of shit."

Danny smiled. "You might be right. Maybe O'Reily here does have an ace up his sleeve. What do you think, Scripture? I thought you were the best hitman on the East Coast?"

Anger lowered Scripture's eyebrows. He lashed out, "*I am!*"

The hired gun at the bar could no longer contain himself. He jumped up and blurted. "That's bullshit, you a muthafucking lie. Everybody out East knows my rep."

Scripture started laughing. "Yo rep? Yo rep? Ain't that about a bitch? I take this little young nigga under my wings, teach him the ropes, and this the respect I get?"

O'Reily felt as though his world was ending. "What the *fuck* is this?"

Danny walked over to O' Reily and removed his gun from his holster. "See, I figured you would figure that I would *figure* you wouldn't come in here alone or without some kind of insurance. So you purposely planted ringers in here so you wouldn't be out of character. I mean, that was a given. But after we got word from Ms. Bedford, we did get your boy off the plane and had him put on ice. We had Scripture's little brother fly in and take his place."

O'Reily took a closer look at the hired gunman and he did look like a younger version of Scripture. How could he have been so *dumb*? "And all this for what? This means nothing; I am untouchable in this city."

Danny pats him on the shoulder. "Seriously O'Reily? Anybody can get touched. What else would it be for? Chicago, the unions, and the heroin market. We knew it was only a matter of time before your Mick cracker ass would come and try to weasel your way in on what we built, so we beat you to the draw."

O'Reily now ready to flex his mob muscle. "You a never get away with this!"

Danny pats Kenneth O'Reily's face. "Don't be a sore looser, lad, Melvin."

The hired hit man pulled out a gun and shot O' Reily right between the eyes. He fell back in the chair, hitting the floor with a loud thud. Blood oozed from his mouth.

The hitman stood over the body. "*Checkmate!*"

* * *

THE PROPOSITION

D anny was sitting in his office when Wallace and the Irishman barged inside. Danny jumped up in anger!

"What the fuck is this?"

Wallace flashed a gun. Danny paused. The Irishman said, "Don't get up on my account."

"What the fuck? I don't keep money here," Danny said.

"I don't want money. I came here to talk business."

Danny was still upset that they had stormed in and caught him off guard, but he sat down. "Next time call and make an appointment."

"Excuse my mannerisms. May I sit?"

"I don't give a fuck what you do, but tell that *motherfucker* to get that piece out my face."

The Irishman took a seat across from Danny.

"Wait in the hall."

Wallace exited the office closing the door behind him.

The Irishman stood at six-feet-five inches and weighed two-hundred-fifty pounds with a thin frame. Jet black wavy hair, a thick mustache, and a strong Irish accent.

Danny.

"What's up?"

"Here's the situation, Kenneth O'Reily was my cousin."

Danny thought, *Here goes the bullshit*. "Yeah and?"

"By law, you should be fucking dead."

Danny answered nonchalantly. "But I'm still breathing and ..."

"And I thought it would be better for everybody involved if we became business partners than if I kill you and yours. Then, some more of yours come and try to kill some of mine, and so on and so on. I mean, it's just a waste of time and money."

Danny relaxed a little. "Not to mention *lives*."

"At the least."

"What kind of business? And I'm telling you right now, I ain't for the fucking games. Come at me correct?"

"Of course, nothing less. I hear you are the *Heroin King* of Chicago."

Danny wasn't impressed in the least. "Yeah and?"

"How would you like to be the *King* of the Midwest?"

Danny sarcastically responded, "Just the Midwest, why not the *West Coast, too?*"

"I already got a man on the West Coast. You mind if I smoke?" The Irishman lights a cigar.

"Knock yourself out."

"If it's too much for you, let me know?"

"Not at all, but why me?"

"Let's say it was this or death. I mean, Kenneth was my cousin and I can forgive and forget for the right price, of course?"

"Of course, how much are we talking?"

"Let's say I front you the first hundred thousand kilos just to see how you do, then we talk in oh two, three months maybe?"

"How long do I have to decide? I got to talk this over with my team."

"I'm sorry, I thought you were the team *captain*, but if you got to get the *okay* then you got to get the okay."

"Look, a hundred thousand kilos ain't a walk in the park, okay?"

"Okay, I hear you. I'll be in town for the night. I leave in the morning. I'll leave my number with your secretary."

The Irishman stood and then exited Danny's office.

* * *

Danny had moved into his father's mansion since his passing. He, Phil-Fine, Scripture, and Randy were all seated in his den.

Danny spoke, "Here's the deal I got. I mean, we got offered a deal earlier today I think we need to move on."

Phil-Fine replied, "Oh yeah, such as?"

"Nine point five million dollars a day deal?"

Scripture now at full attention asked, "Shid, doing what?"

Danny still kept his complete composure. "I got a visit today from O'Reily's cousin, the Irishman. After he left, I had Randy make a few phone calls and have him checked out."

Scripture jumped to his feet marching towards Danny he stood over him, and knelt down so that they were eye to eye. "Yeah, yeah, yeah, get to the nine-point-five million!"

"I'm getting there. Now look, he offered us a chance at running horse through the whole Midwest region."

Phil-Fine shook his head, from side to side angrily in objection. "First off, we haven't got the resources or the manpower to supply the Midwest region. Not to mention the money to buy enough product."

"He said he was going to front us."

Scripture still kneeling down next to Danny stood and began pacing back and forwards. "Front us, how much?"

"A hundred thousand keys."

Phil-Fine shook his head in disbelief, "*A hundred thousand?* A hundred thousand. And what the fuck you think he gonna do when we can't pay?"

"Calm down, little brother."

Phil-Fine felt tension rising, thinking about the problems they may be committing themselves to he unbuttoned the top button of his shirt and loosened his tie. "You calm down. *Shit,* I am calm."

Danny had figured that their responses would be this way. "Look, we ain't doing it unless we all in on it. And not no half-ass shit, either. You with it a hundred percent or not at all. Everybody's vote counts. Especially you, Phil-Fine, with your in-the-game-today-out-tomorrow ass."

Scripture sighed. "Alright, you covered the part about the product, but what about the manpower?"

"We gonna spread ourself-thin, but we got to split up. We all got lieutenants'. Take your lieutenants and hit a spot on the map. Phil-Fine, you take Minnesota, Scripture you and Melvin hit up Detroit, Randy you handle Indiana. As time goes on, we'll get more people and branch out more through St. Louis and Wisconsin and so on and so forth."

Phil-Fine looked at him with astonishment. "You got it all mapped out, huh?"

"Not everything, but we'll work it out together like we always do."

Randy spoke up, "What about you?"

Danny leaned forward so the men could all hear. He spoke in a deadly whisper, "Shit, I'm the *King of Chicago*. I ain't never leaving!"

The End

Excerpts from

Crew Lovept.III

The Final Redemption

Written by
Antwan Floyd

MY WORD IS MY WORD

Those Trenton boys had come along way. Two gang wars, death of loved ones, caused more than their fair share of fatalities! Went from rags to riches and lived to tell about it. So what now?

Danny Trenton the head of his crew would say.

"What you mean? *What now*! The saga continues we get money!"

1960 had ushered in a whole new era and a whole new set of circumstances. After they out smarted O' Reily and seized control of the cities drug trade. In addition to the death of Phil-Good, the eldest son Danny Trenton is now at the helm. He has brokered a deal with O' Reily's cousin The Irishman. He was fronted a hundred thousand kilo's and split the crew up to set up shop in different states through out the Midwest. They still had the numbers thing but that was nothing compared to the money the heroin was bringing in. The crew had changed somewhat Phil-Fine was still in St. Paul clearing nine point five million a week.

Scripture and Melvin still had Detroit doing their numbers with nine in a half a week. Randy was just barely doing four million a week in Indiana, and Lil-Larry was getting his feet wet with a little under seven million a week in St. Louis. Tony and Tim were new to the crew. After the assassination of Phil-Good's right hand man Jermaine Lloyd, Tania eventually moves on and meets a second rate hustler named Nathan Russell. After three months she was pregnant and a month later, he was gone. She gave birth to twin boys Tony and Tim giving them Jermaine's last name. Then Big Cousin was running the numbers portion of the set-up.

It had been eight years since Phil-Fine had moved to Minnesota. In the first two months of setting up shop in St. Paul he had the city on lock. Sandra stayed in Chicago and Phil-Fine made sure that she was well taken care of. While in St. Paul he had met Phyllis Henderson. She was a nineteen-year-old white girl going to school for nursing not long after they met they began living together.

Scripture had always made the right moves at the right time, but this drug shit was confusing. Not that it was confusing because it was hard but confusing because yeah he had killed men before and would do it again with out thinking twice about it. Nevertheless, this shit was getting under his skin mutha fuckas was low down scavenger mutha fuckas! Making they kids go with out eating and shit. The other day he had smashed a man's face in with a wooden mallet. The man had choked his own mother to where she was nearly UN conscious when she refused to give him any more money.

After walking in and witnessing the act Scripture blacked out and by the time, he came back to his right mind the man's face looked like *raw ground beef!* That wasn't what kept him up at night. It was the fact that the same mutha fucka whose face he smashed in was right back at one of his shooting galleries copping again!

Randy was doing bad he had control of a fucking gold mine and was pissing it all away. It was no way in *hell* he should only be doing four million a week and he was supposedly moving over nine million dollars worth of product. Truth of the matter was he was on his way out. If it had been any one *but* him Danny would've cut his head off and dropped it in the garbage the first time he was five-million dollars short! Danny not only loved Randy like a brother, but he had a code of ethics. Randy was from the old school they had put in work together.

It was going on the third week and it wasn't fair that he kept making everyone else pick up the slack for *his* fuck-ups. Danny was really heart broken about the situation. He had driven to Gary himself and asked around. He found out that Randy had a monkey on his back and was fucking off with a broad that was milking him like a cow. He wanted to give him the benefit of the doubt so he never approached him allowing him time to sort the matter out on his own.

St. Louis, most folks probably think it's fields and cow shit at least that's what Lil-Larry thought until he touched down. He was finally coming into his own this was a *lick* Danny had put him on but that wasn't *shit!* Well it was but his biggest conquest was getting Monique in his corner. He had to put in the work but it was worth it, that day was still fresh in his head it gave him nightmares! He walked up to Short Stack with a loaded shot-gun in broad day light and slugs to the chest blew his insides out through his back.

Danny was a self proclaimed –H- King the days of his father's era of Policy Kings were all but forgotten. If it was up to him and it was, he would continue the legacy! He still had Chicago on lock his connect through the Irishman was still in tact, everything was good. He did not deal with the day to day dealings of having to move the product. He had the headaches of setting up dummy operations and businesses to filter the dirty money he earned. That was a lot more stressful than dealing dope. He had his little cousins Tony and Tim on the front line of the street game. The times had changed so Danny being no fool made the changes he needed to make accordingly. He still owned the Golden Lady but it was no happening place to be only old timers hung out there and played cards and got drunk dancing to the music of the thirties and forties.

***

Tim drives his 1960 black Cadillac through the congested traffic in downtown Chicago. He pulls up to a red light and stops. Before he can come to a complete stop good his passenger door was yanked open and Betty with a bright smile jumps in and slams the door closed. Betty is his girl friend she stands at five feet five inches and weighs a hundred twenty pounds strawberry blonde hair and a rose colored complexion. She throws her arms around his neck as the light turns green and he pulls off.

She kisses him on the cheek and leans back in her seat. They make small talk and twenty minutes later they are pulling up in front of a new night-club called Heaven's Gate.

Tim was a local celebrity every body knew him and those that didn't knew of him and wish they did know him. He parks his car in the middle of the street and leaves the engine running. He gets out of the car and walks around to Betty's door and opens it. As she climbs out he closes the door behind her and pinches her soft little butt tucked snug inside the fire red dress that she was wearing.

She smiles, keeps strutting heading towards the entrance to the club. The line is literally down the block to get inside the club. Music can be heard from inside the place. The bouncer at the door immediately recognises Tim and Betty approaching and signals for one of the other bouncers who rushes to the street hopping in Tim's car to go and park it.

The bouncer clears a path for Tim and Betty to enter as they both enter the club.

Tim shakes the bouncer's hand.

"Thanks a lot Troy."

The bouncer opens his hand and places the hundred-dollar bill Tim has slipped him into his pocket.

"No, thank you Mr. Lloyd and enjoy your evening."

Heaven's Gate was the most happening spot in the city they played the best music and they still had a touch of old school on some nights live bands still played.

The finest women in the state came here coming up from Peoria, Harvey, and Park Forrest you never knew what you might get into at Heaven's Gate. Tim and Betty had been seated in the back of the club in a private booth it was Tim's regular seat he liked to see everyone who entered the club he even had a full view of the kitchen. Tim stood at six feet even weighing two hundred pounds he wore his hair in a low cut sported a mustache and goatee he kept looking immaculately shaved and a light skinned complexion.

Twenty minutes later Randy enters the club and joins them at the table. Randy was a former shell of himself standing at almost seven feet tall he was even thinner than he was twenty years before. Weighing a mere hundred forty pounds his clothes fell off him. He still tried to keep up his appearance but he was barely able to do so.

"What's happening little cousin?"

Tim happy to see him smiles.

"Shit how you doing man? I heard you was back in town."

Randy feeling embarrassed.

"Yeah well you know *nothing* lasts forever."

Tim smiles but thinking to himself that would never be him.

Randy continues.

"Can I get a word with you alone?"

Tim looks over at Betty who was already looking at him to see if he wanted her to leave the table or not she was very obedient that way. Tim gives her the eye contact that silently told her that it was ok to stay.

Truth of the matter was Tim already knew what he wanted. Danny had already put the word out not to fuck with Randy on the business side of things if he asked for money or something they were to give it to him but no talk of business!

Tim smiles.

"What is it cousin? You can talk she been trained."

Randy not being one to hold his tongue shrugged his shoulders.

"Tim man you looking for trouble fucking with this broad man!"

Betty's face instantly became red from embarrassment and Tim's face was covered in anger.

"What are you talking about?"

"Come on man, what you think don't nobody know that's *Union Jack's* wife and the *Irishman's* granddaughter?"

"Get out *my* business."

"Listen um telling you this cause I love you this bitch going get *you killed* and fuck up Danny deal he got going if *he don't get killed too!*"

Tim jumps to his feet yelling with spit flying from his mouth as he spoke.

"I'm going let that *bitch* remark slide but I ain't telling you again stay out my business and fuck a Union Jack and a Irishman. DON'T no OTHER nigga tell me who I stick my dick in not Union Jack, not the Irishman, not Danny and especially not no strung out *junkie!*"

A lump formed in Randy's throat as he forced back the tears he turned and exited the club.

***

Danny, June Bug, Tony, Tim, and Big Cousin all sit in Danny's living room he has moved into his father's house. Tony was a spitting image of his brother they even wore the same style hair cut only their mother could tell the two apart. Big Cousin wasn't really their cousin he was just a child hood friend of the twins it was a nickname. He stood at six feet five inches, weighed three hundred fifty pounds, brown complexion, and pearly white teeth with a gap in the front that when he smiled it looked as though he had a tooth missing.

Danny says.

"Listen boys I had a talk with Randy last night."

Tony says.

"Yeah."

"He told me about last night Tim."

"Look Danny man."

Danny cuts him off.

"No you look you was out of line for coming at him like that, completely disrespectful. But you a man just like him and that's all I got to say on that, but as far as that shit with your little lady friend."

Tim cuts him off.

"You ain't even got to say it Danny I got it under control."

Danny laughs.

"You got it under *control?* If I know, don't you think they know? Don't jeopardise the whole crew over somebody else pussy!"

"I know, I know, I know, I got it under control."

Danny leans back in his chair and looks back at Tim with uncertainty in his eyes.

"Alright but don't fuck up this how we *all* eating it ain't just you!"

They all stand up and hug one another.

Tony says.

"Don't worry cuz uma keep a eye on him."

***

Tim was sitting at home alone laying out his out fit he was planning to wear for the night. He was planning to hit Heaven's Gate he was thinking about what Danny had said earlier that day. Was he really risking the entire crew? He shook it off what ever happened with the Betty, Union Jack situation he could handle it. He was about to get in the shower when the telephone rung. He picks up the telephone and talks into the receiver.

"Hello."The voice on the other end of the telephone is Betty she sounds hysterical.

"Tim I have something I have to tell you."

"What is it?"

Betty sounded as though she was on the brink of tears.

"Tim I'm with *child.*"

Tim doesn't say anything he just listens he didn't want to rush the situation so he paused to see what her next response would be. She just wept then all of a sudden became silent. Tim just listened closer through the phone he could no longer hear her breathing through the phone the sound of furniture being smashed and Betty yelling could be heard.

Tim yelled through the telephone.

"Betty!"

He hears her screaming then the phone goes dead, he slams down the phone and grabs his coat yanking the door open and rushing out as Tony was coming in almost knocking him down.

Tony looking surprised says.

"What's wrong?"

"Nothing."

He yells as he continues out the door hops into his car and speeds off.

***

Betty is lying on the floor balled up in a corner of her living room as Union Jack stands over her with a belt in his hand. He stood at a towering six feet tall, weighed a hundred eighty pounds, black hair and a thick black mustache. He brings down blows across Betty's face and back with so much force if he had swung any harder he would've broken his own arm! The thick leather belt tore into her flesh like a bull whip gashes instantly formed as she let out screams of pain the blood from her wounds bled until her flesh became raw.

***

A day has passed since Tony has last seen his brother. He usually wouldn't worry because they would go for weeks at a time not seeing one another but the way he stormed out had stayed on Tony's mind all night.

"*Fuck!*"

He thought I should've followed him, then he shook it off Tim could handle himself he was worrying for nothing. He walks into the Golden Lady he knew that's where Randy usually hung out he wanted to talk with him they hadn't got a chance to talk since he's been home. He was surprised to see Blue Ball there they all exchange hand shakes and hugs.

Tony says.

"Yall ain't seen Tim have yall?"

Blue Ball.

"Nall I ain't seen him in a couple of weeks."

Randy says.

"I ain't seen him since the night before last why what's up?"

"Shit I just ain't seen him since last night that's all I was looking for him."

Blue Ball.

"You don't think nothing happened to him do you?"

Tony has doubt about his brother being all right it was just a feeling he was getting in his stomach but he didn't want them to worry.

"Hell nall he always be pulling this shit he probably laid up with some broad. But do me a favor if one of yall run into my mama and she ask about him just tell her yeah you spoke to him."

Randy knew Tony was on bullshit.

"Come on young cuz if ain't shit wrong what you want us to lie to yo moms for?"

Tony instantly became upset.

"*Damn* can yall just do this one little thang for me or what?"

Blue Ball.

"Talk to us Tony maybe we can help, is Tim in some trouble or something?"

Tony sensed they weren't going to let up he changed his tone of voice.

"I know, if I need any help on any thing I'll let you know, I promise."

Blue Ball, Tony, and Randy all hug goodbyes.

Randy places his hand on Tony's shoulder.

"You be careful out there ok?"

"I will, see yall a little later on."

***

After stopping by Sylvia's Soul food Emporium and grabbing a quick bite he stops by Mercy Hospital, he had heard Tim say once that Betty was a nurse there. When he arrived, they told him that she had quit. He was really becoming *nervous* now. He thought to himself, *I know* my brother. At least he thought he knew his brother. He wouldn't be fool enough to run off with that bitch would he?

Damn would he? Tony just ain't know, she must have had some good *pussy* or some good *head* he knew from experience pussy a make niggas do some silly shit!

He drove down her block he had ridden with Tim once while he was dropping her off so he remembered how to get there.

"*Fuck!*"

He thought to himself, why couldn't this be the wrong address? But he knew he had the right house he just sat parked there as he thought about his next move staring at the empty house with a for sale sign on the front lawn.

Tony was starting to become unravelled so he stopped by a neighborhood liquor store and grabbed a bottle of whiskey. Cruising down Drexel and sipping his liquor through a brown paper bag. He pulls up to an apartment building and goes inside. The place wasn't exactly a slum but it was a little beneath his taste. The place had a buzzer system to gain access into the building but it wasn't any need to get buzzed in because the door was always open any way.

He walked into the building, walked down the hall to the last apartment, and banged on the door. He waits a few seconds then a voice from the other side of the door is heard. Its Ernestine Taylor one of Betty's girl friends she had hooked the two of them up before. They fucked once or twice but they ain't really hit it off. He knew that if any body knew where Betty was she would the two were tight. Ernestine opens the door and Tony was almost knocked off his feet by her beauty.

She stood at six feet even smooth brown skin a 40 double D chest and full soft lips she kept her hair down which was kind of long stopping in the middle of her back. Tony was feeling himself now the liquor was kicking in. He shook it off thinking he would have to come back through after he found his brother. She did have some *all right pussy*.

Ernestine says.

"What's up?"

Tony smiles.

"Shit how you?"

Ernestine steps to the side and lets him enter he closes the door behind himself.

"Listen sweet heart you ain't heard from Betty lately?"

Ernestine pauses and drops her head in silence.

"It's important if you know some shit you need to put me up on it."

Ernestine looks at Tony with deep brown bedroom eyes.

"She made me promise not to say anything but this is serious."Tony not showing any emotion one way or another.

"Are you going tell me or what?"

"She pregnant all right and her old man *knows* it ain't his!"

"So is she with my brother or what?"

"Honestly I don't know I ain't seen your brother or her I just know this much cause she called and told me.""Where did she call you from?"

"Her place I guess I never asked."

"Where's she staying now?"

"The same place as far as I know."

Tony knew she was lying about where she was but he didn't have the time to try to get the information out of her so he hugged her said his good byes and was out the door.

***

Twenty minutes later on the North Side Tony walks into Vick's a neighborhood bar owned by Lonnie Gillispie right hand man to the Irishman. A no bullshit type of guy from the old school sixty-five year old half-breed Italian Irishman about five seven a hundred forty pounds with a receding hairline. When he spoke you could never tell when he was upset because his facial expression never changed and he never raised his voice a real smooth character.

Tony stuck out like a sore thumb the only colored man in a place filled with white gangsters.

Tony didn't feel timid or afraid he walks up to the bar.

"What's going on Lonnie?"

Lonnie had known the twins through Danny but never really dealt with him on any level socially or business wise.

"Nothing much kid."

"You seen my brother?"

"I don't know, you don't know sometimes people they just *go away*."

"What does that mean?"

"Some things should go unanswered as a matter of fact some questions should never be asked!"

All of the men stand and stare at Tony waiting to put it on him as soon as he made a move that they didn't like.

Tony looks around the room with a devilish smirk.

"Yeah ok."

***

The hours were flying by he'd been driving around town the majority of the day and still ain't found out shit about Tim so he figured he'd check in and see if anybody heard from him yet. He pulls up in front of Big Cousin's and blows the horn. Big Cousin looks out of his living room window he sees that it's Tony so he unlocks the door for Tony to enter. Tony walks in they say their hellos shake hands and hug.

Big Cousin with a stern face says.

"Where you been all day? We been looking for you."

"I ain't got time to go into it I got to get back out here and find Tim."

Big Cousin takes a deep breath and exhales.

"We found Tim."

"You did where the hell he at?"

"They dropped him off at the Golden Lady."

Tony already knew what that meant but he asked anyway.

"*What?*"

"Tony man um sorry."

Tony with tears swelling in his blood shot eyes.

"Who?"

"A couple of Union Jack's boys...Tony man them bitches *castrated* him!"

Tony feels the hate swelling up in his chest and turns to run out the door when Big Cousin grabs him by the arm.

"Danny said come and see him it's important."

Tony became even angrier being man handled by Big Cousin who wasn't trying to hurt him but the tighter Big Cousin gripped him the more upset he became.

"Calm down it's going be all right."

Still struggling Tony pulls his gun on Big Cousin.

"I love you man but if you don't let me go um going *plug yo ass!*"

Big Cousin let him go and Tony storms out jumping into his car and speeding away.

Tony had some shit on his mind. Why the fuck he ain't listen when everybody was telling him leave that bitch alone? Why the fuck he ain't follow him? He knew some bullshit was going happen. He rode with his gun on his lap and a machine gun on the back seat. He pulled up to the house he was looking for. Pulling around to the back and parking in the alley. He climbs up the fire escape and climbs in through the window. He moved with the prowess of a cat sleekly and smoothly.

Quickly and quietly it had been a while but he still had it. Back in his teenage years, he and Tim had made a living burglarising homes. He crept through the living room clenching his .45 calibre automatic. He twists the doorknob to the bedroom to find his victim lying in his bed in nothing but tight leopard skin underwear.

The sight made Tony's stomach turn a grown ass man wearing something that looked like women's underwear. The man wasn't even built for the under pants two hundred seventy pounds the majority of which was fat that was all over the place. Tony stood over the man purposely kicking an empty bottle of whiskey against the wall causing the bottle to crash and break waking the man.

"Hello Drew."

Drew opens his eyes and he pauses, he instantly knew whom the man was he had killed his twin earlier that day! He didn't beg for his life he just closed his eyes and tried to remain calm. Tony forced his gun into Drew's mouth knocking out some of his teeth the blood ran down his chin and tears rolled down the sides of his face dripping into his ears. He opened his eyes and looked into Tony's eyes before he pulled the trigger his face exploded into a pile of bloody flesh and brains on a pillow!

Tony was feeling hungry so he stopped over to a female friend's house and had her fix him something to eat. She wanted him to fuck her but he still had unfinished business to attend to. After wolfing the food down he was out the door. Back to the business at hand and the business was *death!* Ten minutes later he was pulling his car up to Hal's auto shop. He parks and gets out of the vehicle. He walks over to Hal who was five feet eight and two hundred pounds he was an Irishman the youngest of Union Jack's brothers. Drew was the oldest Tim had sent him to his maker he had made up his mind that Union Jack had taken his brother so he would take *all* of his!

"I'll be with you in a minute."

Tony smiles knowing this would be Hal's last day breathing. Hal was on the telephone the place was empty except for the two of them Tony begins to laugh as he thought this is *too* easy. Hal wasn't in *the life* he was a working stiff so he had no idea who Tony was.

Hal hangs up the telephone.

"What can I do for you *boy?*"

Tony smiles.

"Well suh I been havin mo problums out uv dis heah automobile than a farmah trying to put a dress on a one eyed mule!"

Tony knew what the man thought of him so he thought he would amuse himself and humor the poor bastard he would be dead in a few minutes anyway.

Hal had a look of annoyance across his face.

"How'd a colored boy like you get a fine automobile like this here?"

Tony continues with the shucking and jiving dumb nigger role he lets out a big hardy laugh.

"Oh no suh this here ain't my automobile. No suh this heah mistah's automobile and I gon be in a world of trouble if I don't git it back to running and be pickin the mistah and da misses up from the airoplane on time."

Hal thought to himself, dem niggas sho'll is some faithful workers if he ever came into some money he'd have to get him one or two.

"Well get in there boy pop the hood and start her up."

Tony shuffles over to the car, does what Hal tell him to do, and gets back out of the car. Hal sticks his head inside the hood and looks around raising his head.

"There's nothing wrong with this vehicle."

"I'd be mighty obliged if you could look once mo suh I jus knows as soon as I leaves from dis heah place it's gon get to misbehavin again."

Hal shakes his head and looks once more raising his head.

"Look boy ain't nothing wrong with this…"

Before he could finish, his sentence Tony had jabbed a knife into Hal's neck forcing the blade upward through his chin into the roof of his mouth! Hal literally choked on his own words as the blood gushed. His weak attempts to protect himself were a waste of time.

A car pulls up behind Tony's car and blows the horn.

Tony yells out.

"I'll be right there."

He drags Hal's dead body to the back of the garage and drops the body in the office on the floor. He returns wiping Hal's blood from his hands on an oily wash cloth. He walks over to the car.

"I'll be with you in a minute buddy but could you pull out so I can get this other customers car out and take a gander at yours."

He pulls the car back and Tony hops into his car and pulls out. The man pulls his car into the garage and gets out of his car watching as Tony speeds off blowing his horn. The man looks at the fleeing car wondering what was going on. He knew something wasn't quite right so he looks around the empty place for another employee.

When he doesn't see any he walks towards the office and reaches for the doorknob. When he looks down on the floor and sees a bloody foot print Tony had left from stepping in Hal's blood that gushed and spilled to the floor. The man hesitated then opened the door to find Hal lying on the floor with his mouth open and the knife still wedged into his mouth and his face lying in a pool of his own blood!

Tony was on his third bottle of whiskey and was feeling good. Two down two to go. First Drew and Hal next would be Freddy and Union Jack. He was riding pass Smoke's he was about to stop when he saw white boys coming out of the pool hall that looked like white hoods. Therefore, he kept driving hoping no one noticed him driving by.

"*Fuck!*"

He thought to himself. They on to me all ready these next two hits meant it was no room for mistakes!

Tony had heard of Freddy he was a real hot head and would come after him with everything he had. However, it didn't matter now it was no turning back. Either he would be dead or they would be dead no in between! By now, Tony had switched vehicles something inconspicuous he had always been a good tail guy. So he put his skills to the test and followed Freddy.

He had two cars with him one in front of him and one behind him. Tony stayed two blocks away watching the three-car entourage. When they came to a red light Tony crept up closer a block at a time. Once they stopped at another light he pulled up next to Freddy's car and shot into the car hitting Freddy in the face on the first shot!

His face exploded into a mess of blood and torn flesh! This clung to the back of the front seat and plastered all over the windshield.

Tony hit the gas and made the first sharp turn he could make hopping onto the express way. The car following Freddy's gave chase and began shooting at Tony as he weaves in between cars on the expressway. The car continues to follow shooting busting out the window to Tony's car. They pull up to the side of his car and throw a cocktail bomb through the passenger's window. The bomb explodes as Tony crashes into the car in front of him. Tony engulfed in flames pushes the door open and jumps out rolling out the flames in the chaotic express way traffic.

The white gangsters continue to drive speeding away from the scene of the crime. A semi-truck swerves out of the way from all most running Tony over and causes another accident. The vehicles behind the truck come to a complete stop causing a forty-car pile up. Tony manages to climb to his feet and limps to a car with a nosy spectator so he pulls his revolver that he kept tucked in an ankle holster. He gets into the car with his gun wedged into her face he orders the woman to drive!

***

Danny, Randy, The Irishman and Wallace all sit in Danny's office at the Sanitation Company.

The Irishman says.

"The thing with Jack's brothers interferes with our arraignment hand over Tony and all is forgiven."

Danny says.

"I don't know where he is?"

The Irishman sounded like he was giving a direct order.

"Find him!"

Danny knowing this wasn't a good time to make a stance.

"I'll get back with you."

The Irishman and Wallace both exit the office as Randy pours a brandy for himself and Danny.

Randy says.

"You not going hand over the kid are you?"

"Hell nall I got his hot head ass hid out until I straighten this thing out."

***

It had been four months since all that shit went down with Tony and Union Jack. It wasn't over though they were still looking for him. He had been hiding out at Ernestine's since that day on the express way when that woman he pulled the piece on dropped him off. She was terrified until he gave her five hundred dollars to keep her trap shut. She relaxed and took him where he wanted to go.

Danny was paying Ernestine two hundred bucks a day to keep Tony laid up until they sorted this whole mess out. Tony was starting to become impatient with the situation. It was taking Danny too long to sort it out with the Irishman. It was a regular day at least for him anyway. Ernestine had just come in from work. She was about to cook dinner when there was a knock at the door.

Tony steps into a closet and pulls out his gun.

Ernestine yells through the door.

"Who is it?"

"It's Betty."

Ernestine quickly opens the door and Betty rushes in. Tony continues to listen through the closet door.

"What are you doing here?"

"I'm leaving Jack I can't take it any more!"

"*You*...you're leaving Jack? After all that's happened *now* you decide to leave?"

"I need a favor?"

"Yes anything!"

Betty opens the door to the hall and returns carrying a baby in a basket.

Ernestine steps back against the wall in shock.

"*Oh my God!*"

"I can't run with him I'll come back as soon as I can."

"Is it *Tim's* baby?"

Betty starts crying uncontrollably and forces out the words.

"Yes."

Tony steps out of the closet startling Betty clutching her new-born son tighter she stares at Tony with shock.

"*What are you still doing in the city?* If they find you..."

He cuts her off.

"They won't and I'm taking my brothers baby and raising him myself. What's, what's his name?"

Betty steps closer to Tony and uncovers the baby's face.

"Timothy Lloyd Jr."

She hands the baby to Tony.

"Keep him safe I don't know what Jack will do if he..."Before she could finish her sentence the door is kicked in and the room is flooded with police and two of Union Jack's men. Before Tony could squeeze off a shot he was clubbed by the police and beaten until he couldn't move. His jaw was broken in three different places and his wrist fractured as blood poured from his skull he was cuffed and drug out of the apartment. One of Jack's men grabs Betty by the neck and forces her to come with them.

"Let's go Union Jack's waiting on you."

The other henchman working for Union Jack.

"What about the baby?"

Ernestine scoops up the baby from the floor, which Tony had dropped and covered with his body from the police who probably would've killed him out of spite.

"You're not touching this child!"

The man in a cold and unusual tone spits out.

"Leave it let her keep the *half breed mongrel!*"

***

Two days later Union Jack and the Irishman ride in a limousine talking about the recent incidents.

The Irishman says.

"I understand about it being embarrassing with Betty and *the nigger* and I know she's your wife but she's my grandchild so the beatings...stop it or leave her! The situation with Danny and his crew they will continue to distribute through out the Midwest."

Union Jack instantly becomes in raged yelling as he spoke.

"Letting those niggers continue to breathe is a spit in my face!"

"Let it go it's not your call your reacting out of anger, one of the boys is dead and the other is in jail for the next thirty years which in most cases is worst than death. Enough is enough the conversation is done!"

***

June Bug had been Danny's unofficial right hand man ever since they started the thing with the Irishman and he had to send Randy to set up shop in another state. June Bug stood at five feet seven and was light skinned with red hair and red facial hair and light freckles that covered his face he weighed a hundred eighty pounds. He was making his drop to one of the Irishman's people as he did every month. Everything was going as usual when a car pulled up and started shooting it all happened before either of the crews knew what happened.

First the two men working for the Irishman went down and the men continued firing next hitting the other man working for Danny. June Bug tried to squeeze off a shot but was unsuccessful as the bullets hit him rapidly in the chest and stomach he fell to the ground screaming in agony. The gunmen run over to the bloody carcasses on the ground and take the money hopping in the car and speeding away from the scene of the crime.

***

Later on that night Danny sits in June Bug's hospital room next to his bed he had surgery earlier that day and it looked like he was going to pull through.

June Bug struggled to speak.

"It was a inside job it was white boys that hit us it had to be the Irishman's people."

Danny had the same thoughts but he couldn't put this pass June Bug either he doesn't say anything he just pats June Bug on the shoulder and exits the hospital. He crosses the street and gets into the back of the Irishman's limousine where he is waiting.

The Irishman in a calm and cool voice spoke with a deathly tone.

"I want my money!"

Danny truly confused responded.

"What in the hell are you talking about? My guy is the one in the hospital from a bullet in his stomach from one of your people. I thought you was above petty scams but I ain't paying twice."

The Irishman now with anger in his voice shouts.

"You have a guy in the hospital two of my guys lying on a cold slab in a morgue and they ain't find no money on the body! So who am I to believe the one's who dead with no money on them? Or the one who breathing with a bullet in him?"

Danny really letting his emotions get the better of him as the veins pop out of his neck he barks at the Irishman.

"So that's thirty-million dollars that's just gone?"

The Irishman looked surprised.

"*Thirty-million dollars?*"

"Yeah fifth-teen for this month and fifth-teen for next month."

"Fifth-teen or thirty I ain't taking the lost you have one week to make up the difference now get out of my car!"

***

The next morning as the Irishman and Union Jack ride in the back of the limousine on their way to the country club for breakfast.

Union Jack laughs.

"You should've let me take care of this like I said."

"It doesn't make sense I've been dealing with these men for almost ten years now, they pull this for what *peanuts?*"

"Yeah just like niggers a *lousy* thirty-mil"

The Irishman pauses.

"*What did you say?*"

"They blow a sweet deal for a lousy thirty-mil."

The Irishman shrugs his shoulders.

"Well he has a week to pay me if not...well anyway I want you to do it personally."

***

A week has gone pass since Danny had the conversation with the Irishman he is on his way to the hospital to visit June Bug. Big Cousin drives.

Danny says.

"You been up to see Tony?"

"Once, he said he ain't want no visitors at least not right away."

"Good how's the baby?"

"He doing real good I got attached to him quicker than I thought I would. How you going handle the Irishman thing?"

"*Fuck* the Irishman he don't want to have a war of the wits I've outsmarted men like him before and he should be no different."

They pull up to the hospital.

"You want me to come up?"

"No relax I should be fine I won't be too long."

Big Cousin stays in the car as Danny gets out and walks into the hospital. He walks into June Bug's room just as he has finished getting dressed he's about to be discharged. Danny smiles and shakes his hand Danny pulls him close laughing they embrace in a strong hug and June Bug plunges a knife into Danny's back. The pain is so severe that although Danny opened his mouth a scream never came out.

He stammered to get the words out.

"*Why?*"

"Fifty-thousand dollars is a lot of money!"

He twists the knife in his back and pushes Danny's dead body to the floor stepping over him and exiting the hospital room.

Ten minutes away from the hospital Union Jack rides with Lonnie on their way to the hospital as they pull up to the hospital they see Danny's car parked out front.

Lonnie says.

"I told you he was here."

"Wait here it'll only take a second."

Union Jack gets out of the car and walks into the hospital and goes straight to June Bug's room to find Danny lying dead on the floor in a pool of his own blood. He returns to the car laughing as he climbs back into the passenger seat.

Lonnie looked confused.

"What in the hell is so funny?"

"Son of a bitch somebody beat me to the draw he already *dead!*"

"I know."

"What?"

"The Irishman was hurt by your actions he never told nobody about the thirty-mil so how did you know?"

Union Jack had a look of a man who's been caught in a lie about infidelity by his wife.

"*What?*"

No sooner than the word escaped his mouth there was a tapping on the window where Union Jack was seated he turns and looks out the window just as the trigger was pulled ripping his face open. June Bug drops the gun and calmly walks to a parked car with the engine running. Gets in and drives off. Big Cousin who had by this time had pulled off once he heard the gunshot never even saw June Bug exit the hospital. Lonnie gets out of the car just as the Irishman's limousine was pulling up he gets into the car with the Irishman and the driver drives on.

Lonnie slouches in his seat.

"Why still hit Danny if you knew it was Union Jack all along?"

"It wasn't personal it was strategic every one knew he owed me money. I gave my word he would die in a week if I wasn't paid.

I can't start breaking my word being that I'm getting old it makes me look weak it isn't good for business!"

***

ABOUT THE AUTHOR

Antwan Floyd Sr. is an American novelist, most widely recognized for his crime fiction. He has written a series of best-selling mysteries featuring the hard-boiled detective Black Love, a black private investigator living in Chicago, IL; they are perhaps his most popular works.